Scale
of the
Dragon

Marked by the Dragon Book 1

RICHARD FIERCE

Dragonfire Press

Copyright © 2021 Richard Fierce

All rights reserved. All events portrayed in this book are fictitious, and any resemblance to real people or events is purely coincidental. All rights reserved, including the right to reproduce this book or portions thereof in any form without the express permission of the publisher.

Cover design by germancreative.

Cover art by Rosauro Ugang

ISBN: 978-1-947329-72-0

CONTENTS

Map	i	Chapter 11	71
Chapter 1	1	Chapter 12	78
Chapter 2	8	Chapter 13	85
Chapter 3	15	Chapter 14	91
Chapter 4	23	Chapter 15	98
Chapter 5	29	Chapter 16	104
Chapter 6	37	Chapter 17	111
Chapter 7	43	Chapter 18	118
Chapter 8	49	Chapter 19	123
Chapter 9	57	Chapter 20	130
Chapter 10	65	Chapter 21	135

MAP

1

The sun glared overhead, reminding Mina why she dreaded Lord Klodian's summer hunting trips. He was almost obsessive in his desire to hunt dragons for sport, and he used Mina like a hound to sniff them out.

Her life hadn't always been so exciting. Once, she'd been a normal girl that worked the farm with her family … until they sold her to Lord Klodian. Those days seemed so long ago now. At least the memories no longer brought her to tears. She'd cried enough to last her the rest of her life, as far as she was concerned.

"Which way, girl?"

Mina's pace had slowed, prompting Lord Klodian's demand. She looked over her shoulder at him. He sat astride his black warhorse, his polished plate armor glinting in the sunlight. The visor of his helm was up, and he glared at her impatiently.

To his right rode a group of his retainers, and on his left was Vhan, Klodian's squire. The retainers stared at her with a bored expression plastered on their faces, but Vhan looked excited. The squire was always thrilled when it came to dragon hunts.

"This way," Mina replied.

She continued trudging along the dunes, following the subtle pull she felt from the scale embedded in her leg. It infuriated her that Klodian forced her to walk while he and his entourage got to ride horses. Certainly, he knew it would be quicker if she were mounted, but then again, he probably did it just to spite her.

Mina was Klodian's slave, and she knew it. Whether or not it was legal was another issue, but from what Mina had gathered so far in her young life, Dominion Lords did whatever pleased them so long as it didn't get them into trouble with the High Prince.

She supposed it was a small blessing to belong to Klodian. There were rumors that other Dominion Lords could be very abusive, violent even. While Klodian had never raised a hand toward her, he was manipulative and impetuous. Growing up amidst the wealthy and elite seemed to breed those qualities into people, though.

Ahead, Mina spotted a tall mesa that rose several hundred feet above the surrounding landscape. The top was flat, and the sides were steep and straight as if some underground creature had pushed it directly up out of the ground. The rock formation was various shades of red all intermingled, but that wasn't what caught Mina's attention.

It was the shadowed cave entrance.

She angled her steps toward the mountain and the scale in her leg began to burn. It was only slightly uncomfortable, but once they got within a few hundred feet of the dragon, the pain would be excruciating. It happened every time, but that never stopped her. It wasn't the fear that Klodian would punish her that kept her from turning away. It was her hatred for dragons.

They were the source of her misery. Or rather, one of them was. That didn't matter to Mina. The only good dragon was a dead one, and so she would continue to lead Lord Klodian on his hunts with the hope that—one day—he would kill the beast whose scale made her life a nightmare.

"It's there," Mina said. "Inside the cave."

"You're certain?" Klodian asked. "It's not on top, preparing to swoop down on us?"

She turned to regard him. Klodian hadn't kept his title as Dominion Lord for no reason. He'd been born to the position, certainly, but that didn't guarantee someone the title for life. There was always some young upstart who wanted the power and fame for themselves, and Klodian's quick wits and suspicion had saved him from many assassination attempts.

"I'm certain, my Lord. The scale may be a curse, but it never lies."

"One man's curse is another man's godsend. You may not like your ability, girl, but your gift has increased my wealth fourfold."

That was another thing that bothered Mina. Lord Klodian always referred to her as 'girl' and never by her actual name. She supposed he did that out of spite, as well.

"You are entitled to your opinion, as am I. And I

say it is a curse."

Klodian laughed and slid off his mount, landing with a clatter as his plate mail jounced about. He unsheathed his sword from his waistbelt and quickly looked it over, then returned it. He motioned to Vhan, and the squire also dismounted. Vhan carried a spear, but the weapon wasn't his. He hadn't earned the privilege of learning to fight yet.

"Wait for me out here," Klodian ordered, taking the spear from Vhan. "I'll be back shortly."

Mina watched him disappear inside the cave. The retainers began talking amongst themselves, sharing gossip and discussing things that made Mina wish a dragon would swoop down on them. Whether it ate them or her didn't matter, so long as it put her out of her misery.

Vhan slowly sidled around to where Mina stood, a grin on his face.

"Don't even ask," Mina said.

"I've never seen it," Vhan replied. "And I *really* want to see it."

"Why? So you can make fun of me, too? No, thank you."

"I wouldn't make fun of you. I think having a dragon scale in your leg is neat. I'd have one if I could. How did you get that, anyway?"

"I'm sure you've heard the stories," Mina said.

"I've heard rumors, which is usually far from the truth. And I've never heard the story from you, so …"

Vhan stared at her expectantly.

"I fell on it."

"Care to elaborate?"

Mina heaved a sigh, knowing Vhan would irritate her until she gave in.

"I was playing in the hills when I was young, and a hole opened up beneath me. I fell into a dragon's nest and landed on a pile of scales. This one," Mina slapped her thigh, "happened to penetrate my skin."

Vhan's eyes were wide. "Seriously? That must have been amazing. Being in a dragon's nest, I mean."

"The nest was abandoned. And it wasn't amazing at all. It ruined my life."

"You're alive, aren't you?" Vhan asked.

"I exist, but I wouldn't exactly call being a slave to Klodian living."

"Some people don't like him, but I do. He's always nice to me. I have a warm bed and food to eat, so I can't complain. There wasn't much to go around at my home, so being the squire to Lord Klodian has been the best thing that's happened to me."

Mina offered him a fake smile in the hopes that he'd get the hint and stop talking, but he kept yammering on about how great it was to be part of Klodian's Dominion. Mina tuned his voice out and watched the cave entrance, wondering how long it would take Klodian to kill the dragon. Her leg was still burning, which meant it wasn't dead yet. At least he hadn't forced them to go into the cave with him.

After a while, Vhan left her alone and wandered over to listen to the retainers. Mina rubbed her leg, massaging the skin around the edges of the scale. She didn't fear for Klodian's safety. If he died, then she'd have an opportunity to escape. It wasn't likely he'd be killed, though. Not when he had the power of his runes. That was another perk the wealthy nobles enjoyed: magic.

Rune magic was sanctioned by the High Prince, and it was only lawful for nobles to employ it. Everything else was outlawed, but that didn't stop people from practicing it in secret. Although Mina had never met any illegal sorcerers, she knew they were out there. It was whispered that on the fringes of the Dominions, there were people who openly sold their services to others.

The burning in Mina's leg ceased abruptly, and she smiled. Another dragon was dead. *Good riddance,* she thought. A moment later, Lord Klodian stepped out from the cave. He was covered in dust and blood, and he carried a severed horn in one hand. Vhan rushed over and fawned over him, ever the loyal squire. Mina found the display annoying and turned her gaze away, looking up at the mesa's jagged walls.

"That's the first dragon of the season," Vhan said.

"The first of many," Klodian replied. "Girl."

Mina looked at him, and he tossed the horn to her. She caught it and turned it over, examining it. It was small, and she guessed the dragon must have been an adolescent.

"For your collection," Klodian said.

"Thank you, my Lord."

"Ride back to the castle and summon the workers," Klodian instructed Vhan. "Tell them to bring plenty of wagons. The beast was hoarding enough trinkets to fund an army."

"Right away, sir."

Vhan got on his horse and rode off. The retainers gathered around Klodian and listened to him relay how he killed the dragon. Mina ran her fingers along the horn, feeling the coarse lines that grooved its surface. Every horn was different, but they all had similarities. She glanced at the cave and thought she saw glowing eyes staring back at her from the shadows. She blinked a few times and squinted, but there was nothing there.

It was probably her imagination. She waited for Klodian to finish bragging about his kill, and then they began the trek back to the castle. Mina clutched the horn in her hands, hoping that the next dragon to be killed would be the one to set her free.

How she hated dragons.

2

It had been a grueling day for Caden.

He'd faced a series of challenges that tested both his mind and his body, and he'd pushed his limits further than he ever believed possible. Feats of strength, tactical challenges, and many other trials meant to determine whether he was worthy of being a Runesman had been his sole focus.

And he'd made the cut.

Caden stood in line, waiting for his turn to be marked. A few of his fellows had suffered minor injuries, and the man in front of him was bleeding from a cut on the back of his head. It didn't seem to bother him, so Caden didn't point it out.

Both exhausted and dirty, Caden was ready to rest. The challenges had been physically taxing, true, but his mind had been tested even harder. He'd tried to only think about his tasks, but that hadn't helped. The entire time he'd been questioning himself, worried that he'd fail somehow. When given the news that he'd been accepted as a Runesman, it was as if a heavy weight had been lifted from his shoulders.

If there was one thing that Caden wanted in life, it was fame. And riches. So, two things. They usually came hand in hand, anyway. He didn't want to be a Dominion Lord—and couldn't be one—but he *did* want everything they had. And the easiest way to gain both was to become a Runesman.

Since he lived in the Thophate Dominion, that meant that he'd been forced to enlist in Lord Ardit Klodian's army. That wasn't necessarily a problem in itself, but Lord Klodian didn't wage war against the other Dominions enough for Caden to earn the renown he wanted. So, he'd devised a plan. A plan of simplicity that had little chance of failing in his mind.

He would enlist with Lord Klodian, then request a citizen's transfer to another Dominion. Transferring to another Dominion wasn't unheard of, and with the right coaxing, there would be no reason Lord Klodian should refuse him.

The only flaw Caden could find with his plan was that he didn't know which Dominion was in good standing with Lord Klodian. They fell in and out of favor with one another as often as the wind changed direction, which meant that Caden would have to keep his ears open. If he requested a transfer to one of Klodain's enemies, well … that would be bad.

"Step forward."

A portly middle-aged man sat behind a wooden table, scrawling names onto a parchment with a feather-pen. He dipped the quill into an inkwell and gazed up at Caden. The man wore thin spectacles, and they hovered at the edge of his nose, threatening to slip free at any moment.

"Name?"

"Caden Davtyan," Caden said.

The man repeated the name under his breath as he wrote Caden's name down, misspelling his surname. Caden didn't bother correcting him. No one had ever managed to spell his surname properly, and Caden's father had taught him long ago that a man must pick his battles carefully.

"Do you own a blade?"

"Not yet," Caden replied, giving the man a grin.

"Right then. Go to the red tent where those men are and wait for Captain Eduard. He'll determine the best rune for you."

"Thank you."

Caden strolled over to the tent the steward had motioned to, joining the group of men waiting there, and glanced around the field. They were outside the castle, and various obstacles had been set up for the day's festivities. Enlistment day only came around once every few months, and Caden had waited a long time for this moment. Now that the Runesmen had been chosen, servants were working on clearing the field.

Turning his attention to the other members of his group, Caden spotted a man with long braided hair. He thought it was odd until the man turned around and he realized it wasn't a man at all, but a woman.

"What are you looking at?" she snapped.

"Nothing," Caden answered calmly. He didn't

avert his eyes, though. He matched her stare.

"You don't think I should be here, do you? Well, I've got just as much right to be here as you. And I guarantee I could kick your butt across this field without breaking a sweat."

"Calm down, Thais," one of the others said. "Save your energy."

"Shut your mouth," Thais growled back at him. "Or I'll pummel you, too."

She shot Caden another glare before turning away. Caden shook his head, finding it funny that a woman would want to join the Runesmen. He supposed she had her reasons, just as he did, and that he shouldn't look down on her.

Captain Eduard, an imposing man decked out in chainmail and leather armor, strode over to the tent and began assigning people their runes. Some of them left to other tents, but Caden and a handful of others were instructed to stay where they were.

"Each of you showed proficiency in many areas, but those of you standing here excelled at one thing in particular. Strength."

Captain Eduard looked at each of them, meeting their gaze for a moment before looking to the next person.

"Being a Runesman is something most envy, but not everyone is cut from the same cloth. Some of your fellows will be marked for sight, and others for speed. Though you may have different runes, you are all a brotherhood dedicated to the same cause.

Defend the Thophate and protect Lord Klodian. Do you all swear allegiance to your new lord until the day you die?"

"I swear it," Caden said, his voice joining the chorus of his fellows.

"Good. The Marking will hurt, but only for a short while. It burns more than anything, at least it did for me. Remove your shirts and take a seat. The scribes will perform their work, and then you will be escorted to the barracks."

Caden removed his shirt and stuffed it into his belt. Everyone else removed theirs as well, except for Thais. She stood rooted in place, her face a mask of stoicism.

"Is there a problem?" Captain Eduard asked.

Thais cleared her throat. "Must I remove my shirt?"

"If you want to be a Runesman. Are you having second thoughts?"

"No, sir."

Caden eyed her from his peripheral, wondering if she was actually going to go through with it. After a brief moment of hesitation, she removed her shirt. Thais's jaw tightened and Caden knew if anyone said anything inappropriate, she wouldn't hesitate to lay them out on their back.

No one said a word.

Everyone took a seat upon a wooden chair. The chairs were designed differently than anything

Caden had seen before, with the back of the chair actually being in the front. The design allowed the person sitting to lean forward, and as Caden did so, he understood the idea behind the design.

A group of elderly men joined them under the tent, and each one carried a bucket filled with supplies. Caden's scribe set his bucket down and removed clean strips of cloth, inkwells, and some sort of metal instrument. He laid them out on the table and used one of the cloth strips to cleanse a spot on Caden's back, just below his neckline.

None of the scribes spoke as they worked. Caden gritted his teeth against the pain as sharp pinpricks stabbed the flesh along his spine. And it burned, just as Captain Eduard had said it would. From his side view, Caden watched another scribe work on Thais. Her eyes were closed, but she flinched here and there as the old man stabbed her with his metal instrument.

He dipped the tip of it into an inkwell, then jabbed it into Thais's flesh. As far as Caden could tell, each scribe followed the same process. While he knew that being a Runesman granted his lord the ability to borrow an attribute, he knew nothing about how the magic of the runes actually operated.

As he watched the scribe work, he assumed the magic imbued within the rune had something to do with the ink being used. The scribes were tattooing a rune into their flesh, and since that rune connected them to their lord, it seemed logical to Caden that the ink was magical in some way.

Thais opened her eyes and glanced at him, scowling. Caden turned his gaze straight ahead and tried not to think about Thais beating him to a pulp. He also tried not to think about her naked upper half, as that would cause other problems. She reminded him of a feral animal, wild and dangerous. And yet, he was attracted to her. She was pretty, there was no denying that, but her personality clashed with her looks enough that Caden knew he'd never pursue anything with her.

His conflicting thoughts were interrupted as a sharp pain lanced down his back, and he felt his feet go numb. The scribe tattooing him slathered something thick and greasy onto his flesh, rubbing it in thoroughly. The numbness faded, but his back still burned like fire.

"The rune is complete," the old man said.

Caden sat up, stretching the stiffness from his muscles. He watched the old man place everything back into his bucket, and then he left. Captain Eduard came over to inspect the rune and nodded his approval.

"Well done, Runesman."

Caden couldn't help but grin like a fool.

3

When the red stone walls of Klodian Keep came into view, Mina breathed a sigh of relief. She'd had the feeling that someone was watching them. The idea was ludicrous, she knew, but the feeling was intense. Lord Klodian and his retinue were oblivious, still talking about his prowess in killing the dragon from the mesa.

Even Vhan wasn't paying attention to their surroundings. Granted, they were within the boundaries of the Thophate Dominion, but that didn't mean that enemies weren't lurking, waiting for a chance to eliminate Lord Klodian. Mina rubbed at the scale on her leg absently and wondered whether the glowing eyes she had seen had truly just been her imagination.

It was hot and she was thirsty, so maybe she had seen a mirage. The more she considered it, the more she became convinced that's what it had been. As they got closer to the castle, Mina could see that Enlistment Day was nearing an end. Klodian customarily watched over the proceedings, but today had been different.

Klodian and the others rode at a slow pace, allowing Mina to keep up with them. He usually left her behind, knowing that she would eventually make her way back to the castle. Vhan occasionally looked back at her, and she assumed he was checking on her. Vhan seemed like a nice person, but Mina had learned long ago not to trust anyone.

When they reached the field where the newest Runesmen were, Klodian stopped and dismounted. Vhan hurriedly followed suit, trailing after the lord like a puppy. Mina kept her distance from them, but she did glance over the faces of Klodian's newest soldiers. She didn't recognize any of them, but she did spot a woman among the mix. That was a first.

"Lord Klodian," Captain Eduard greeted, bowing.

"Captain."

"How was the hunt?"

"It was good," Klodian replied, removing his helmet. "I'll tell you about it later. How many new Runesmen do we have?"

"Sixty."

Mina could tell by the way the Eduard said it that he knew Klodian wouldn't be pleased. The Dominion Lord scanned the sea of new faces and finally nodded.

"Why so few?"

"You have high standards, my Lord. It is my duty to enforce those standards and only enlist the best."

"What of the Marking? Any problems?"

"Three," Captain Eduard answered. "Three died during the process."

Mina was surprised to hear that. It was rare for

anyone to die during the Marking, but it wasn't impossible. Those too weak to accept the magical rune were typically released from their oath and they went on to find another pursuit in life, but with a few new scars. For three to have died … well, the scribes responsible would be put to death as punishment.

Klodian frowned. "I see. How about the assignments?"

"Ten were marked for strength. Five for haste, and five for vision. The rest were given the common rune."

"I needed more footmen, so I'm happy to hear that. Hopefully, we'll see more talent at the next enlistment. Carry on, Captain. I'll see you at the feast tonight."

Klodian and Vhan climbed back onto their horses and returned to the castle, leaving Mina behind. She offered a bow to the captain, but he ignored her and walked off, shouting orders at the servants clearing the field.

Mina regarded the female Runesman curiously. She'd never seen a woman as a soldier, nor had she ever heard of such a tale. The woman returned her stare, fire in her eyes.

"Do you have a problem?"

"No," Mina replied.

"Then why are you looking at me?"

"I'm curious is all. Why would you want to be a

soldier?"

"That's my business," the woman spat. "Keep your nose out of it."

"For Hadon's sake, Thais. Not everyone is your enemy."

The woman named Thais turned to the man who'd spoken and punched him in the face, knocking him to the ground.

"Everyone is your enemy until they prove otherwise," she growled. "And you!" Thais turned back to Mina, her right hand balled into a fist. She took a few steps forward, but another man stepped into her path.

"Just stop," he said.

"Move out of my way unless you want to get thumped next!"

The man crossed his arms and refused to move. The two stared at one another, neither one backing down. Mina's face flushed with embarrassment. No one had ever defended her, and it felt odd to have a stranger do it.

"Please," Mina begged. "I meant no disrespect. Don't fight because of me. I'm leaving now."

"You aren't going anywhere until I bash your face in!" Thais shouted.

"Go cool off somewhere," the man said.

"No one tells me what to do!"

Thais leaped forward, and the two clashed. They

tumbled to the ground and fought, punching and rolling around. Mina watched, horrified. Thais gained the upper hand, pinning the man's arms with her knees. Just as she was about to punch the man in the face, Captain Eduard came rushing over, driving his right knee into the side of Thais's head. Her face scrunched in confusion and she toppled over with a groan.

"Did you so quickly forget your oath?" Captain Eduard demanded. "We are a brotherhood with the same cause. No one here is your enemy. You would do well to remember that."

The captain paused, looking from Thais to the man.

"I think five lashings for the both of you will be a fit reminder. Report to me after dinner. I'll deal with you then."

Captain Eduard stalked off, shooting a glare in Mina's direction. He could have punished her too, with Klodian's approval, but Mina guessed he didn't think it was worth the effort. Mina might be a slave, but she was a valuable one.

Thais slowly rose to her feet and staggered off. The man waited until she was gone, then he sat up and smiled at Mina.

"Sorry about her," he said. "I've only met her today. She's got a bit of a temper."

Mina had been taken aback before, but now doubly so. Not only had a stranger helped her, but he'd fought a fellow Runesman to do it. If the day got anymore strange, she'd have to assume she was dreaming.

"No, it's me that should apologize," Mina replied. "I shouldn't be standing around out here."

"Nonsense." The man got up and brushed a trail of blood from his lips with the back of his hand. "I'm Caden. What's your name?"

"Mina."

Caden's brows rose slightly. "Lord Klodian's fortune finder?" He glanced down at her legs briefly, and Mina knew what he was looking for.

"The same," she answered curtly.

"I apologize, that sounded less rude in my head."

"Don't worry about it. I'm used to it."

Caden was taller than her by roughly a full foot. He was well-muscled and clean shaven, with short brown hair and green eyes. Despite the dirt and grime, Mina found him rather alluring. The silence stretched until it became awkward, and Caden cleared his throat.

"I don't want to start on the wrong foot," he said. "I'm sorry if I offended you. That wasn't my intent."

His tone was sincere, but Mina didn't trust him. He was a stranger, and despite his actions to defend her, she wouldn't let her guard down, no matter how handsome he was.

"All is forgiven," she said. "As I said, I'm used

to it."

She was clutching her dragon horn tightly, feeling uncomfortable. Part of it was her attraction to Caden, but she also still felt as if someone was watching her. She was confident that once she got inside the castle, the feeling would subside.

"I should be going."

"Would you like me to escort you?" Caden asked. "In case Thais hasn't learned her lesson?"

"No," Mina said quickly. "I'll be fine."

She speed-walked across the field, heading to the castle. She could tell her cheeks were flushed by the way they burned. Aside from her discomfort around Caden, she also needed to get the dragon horn to her room so she could take the necessary steps to preserve it. If she waited too long, the horn would dry out from the desert heat and slowly rot from the inside, becoming brittle.

Mina reached her room and barely remembered her trek through the confusing network of hallways. Klodian hadn't built the castle, but he had made several changes to the interior when he'd taken up his father's mantle, transforming it into a literal maze.

He'd claimed it was to make the castle a more formidable fortress, but no one had ever attacked the Thophate Dominion before. It was on the border of The Long Sands, much too far for an enemy army to march to, let alone conquer. The heat itself stopped most people from coming to Thophate, and only merchants and traders with deep pockets braved the trip.

After she'd treated the horn, Mina cleaned herself and changed clothes, then ate the small meal that was delivered to her bed. As she went about her evening tasks, she couldn't help but think of the Runesman from earlier.

"Caden," she whispered, a smile pulling at her lips.

4

After the dark of night had fallen, and he'd received his five lashings, Caden laid on his cot in the barracks, trying not to move much. Even breathing sent pain flaring through his wounds, but he didn't regret his actions.

Thais had been wrong to threaten Mina or anyone else for that matter. She had some serious anger issues, or perhaps someone had deeply hurt her in the past. Either way, Caden wasn't sure how to handle her. He never expected to fight a woman, but she had attacked him. And she would have knocked him unconscious if it weren't for Captain Eduard intervening.

Something creaked, and Caden lifted his head. The barracks were dark, but he saw a shadow moving slowly in his direction.

"Who's there?" he whispered.

"Shut your mouth," Thais's voice whispered back.

Caden laid his head back down and sighed. If she was here to fight him again, he knew he would lose to her. She'd been lashed too, but he thought she handled the pain with much more grace than he had. He chalked it up to her having a higher pain threshold. Thais reached his bed and stood over him. Her face was hidden by the shadows, but her posture didn't seem menacing.

"What do you want?" Caden asked lowly.

"I wanted to apologize for beating you up," Thais replied. "I expected more of a challenge."

"Go away."

There was a brief moment of silence.

"No one has ever stood up to me the way you did."

"That's surprising. You're a bully, Thais. Eventually, someone always puts the bully down."

"I …" She sighed. "Where I come from, soft people die. I had to learn to be tough and trust no one because I didn't want to die. You may not understand that, but it's the truth."

Caden stared up at her shadowy figure, mulling over her words. Perhaps she wasn't as terrible a person as he first assumed.

"You don't have to apologize to me," he finally said. "But you might want to apologize to Mina."

"The girl from earlier?"

"Yes. That's Lord Klodian's girl. The one who leads him to his dragons."

Thais stiffened. "I didn't know. Do you think she'll rat me out to Lord Klodian?"

Caden smiled. He didn't believe Mina would do that, but it wouldn't hurt to keep a little fear in the air. "Possibly. If you apologize quickly, she may let it pass."

"I'll talk to her first thing tomorrow."

"Good idea. Now, can I try to get some sleep?"

Thais climbed onto the cot with him and laid her head on his chest. Caden froze, unsure of what she was doing. She didn't move or try to seduce him, and he eventually relaxed when he realized she had fallen asleep. He decided that Thais was more like a wild animal than he first realized, and it seemed like she needed a friend. And that was something he could be for her if she needed it. Until he transferred Dominions, anyway.

When he awoke the next morning, Thais was gone. Judging by the lack of light coming through the windows, dawn hadn't quite arrived. Caden sat up slowly and was surprised to find that he didn't feel any pain at all from the previous day's punishment. He left the cot and headed for the washroom, where he splashed cold water onto his face. A small mirror hung on the wall, and he removed his shirt and twisted awkwardly to get a look at his back.

The rune was there, an onyx symbol that looked like a pillar. A set of eyes sat between the crossbars of the upper portion, and two swords crossed over the center. The details were intricate, and Caden understood now why the Marking had taken so long. What surprised him, however, was the absence of his wounds.

There was no sign that he'd been lashed at all, not even reddened or upraised flesh. He stared at his back in disbelief. How was that possible?

"Pretty neat trick, huh?"

Caden whirled around to see Thais in the doorway. "What trick?"

"The rune healed our wounds."

"How?"

"Magic, probably. What good would we be as Runesmen if we couldn't heal quickly? The Dominion Lords would have a tough time keeping their ranks full, especially in the Dominions that are always warring with one another."

Caden took a final look at his back and slipped his shirt back on.

"You seem to be in a better mood today," he said, turning to face Thais.

"I got some sleep," she replied, shrugging. "I'm not always a raging b—"

A horn blared outside the barracks, cutting off her words. The main quarters erupted in chaos as people scrambled out of bed, swiftly dressing and rushing out into the courtyard. Caden and Thais hurriedly followed their fellows.

Captain Eduard was standing with his arms clasped behind his back. Instead of his chainmail and leather armor, he was wearing black pants and a brown shirt. An olive-colored cloak draped his shoulders, tied at the neck. Strapped at his waist was a sword with a black hilt, and the pommel was a large clear stone. Once everyone had lined up, Captain Eduard cleared his throat.

"What is the purpose of a Runesman?" he

asked.

"To protect the Dominion and its lord," someone shouted.

"Correct, at least on the surface. If you dig a little deeper, what do you find?"

Silence met his question, and he flicked his gaze across the line.

"I wouldn't expect any of you to know yet, but I'm always hoping for a surprise. We are a brotherhood unlike any other. Are we soldiers? Yes, but we are more than that. We have been given a gift that many will never receive. Having this rune on your body isn't just a sign of who you serve. It's an honor that you uphold.

"Do you know why Lord Klodian made me the captain of his Runesmen? Not simply because I've proven myself to him countless times. It is because I know what it means to be a warrior. And I am going to teach you to be warriors."

Thais raised her hand.

"Yes?" Captain Eduard asked.

"We're already warriors, aren't we? We're here to kill, and I'm sure any of us can do that."

"There's more to being a warrior than killing someone. War without purpose is brutality. We are not tyrants. If that is what you are here for, you can leave now. Listen carefully, all of you. Your first lesson is this: Courage, above all things, is the first quality of a warrior. It takes courage to do the right thing, especially in the face of adversity.

"Beginning tomorrow, you will wake before dawn and run ten laps around the castle. The horn that woke you this morning will blare every morning at the same time. I suggest you do not ignore it unless you enjoy being punished. After you finish your morning run, you can enter the castle for breakfast. You will eat, and you will return here for your training. Are there any questions?"

Caden glanced down the line, but nobody spoke.

"Good. Start running. Ten laps, all the way around. If you don't finish, you don't eat."

Caden wasted no time. He broke from the line and took off, jogging at a swift pace. He made sure not to push himself too hard, fearing that if he was forced to walk at all, he'd be lashed again. A couple of people sprinted past him, but he ignored them and focused on keeping a steady stride. Thais eventually joined him, matching his steps and jogging beside him.

He wasn't sure, but he suspected that she liked him.

5

As a child, Mina's parents never taught her to read. In retrospect, she assumed it was because they didn't know how themselves. They were farmers, after all, and had no use for such privileges.

She stared at the spines of the books as she dusted the shelves they rested upon, wondering what the letters spelled out. The colors of the books varied from black to navy to green, and they were all in pristine condition. This was Lord Klodian's private study, and he demanded only the best.

Mina paused in her work when she spotted a book that had gold lettering. She glanced around, making certain she was alone and pulled the book out. It had some heft to it, and she cracked it open and idly flipped through the pages. Flowing script filled every inch of parchment space. Mina was disappointed to find that there were no pictures.

The sound of approaching footsteps startled her and she quickly replaced the book and continued dusting.

"Where is that blasted girl?" It was Lord Klodian. "Girl!"

Mina rushed toward the open door, reaching it just as Klodian stepped into view.

"I'm here, my Lord."

"Where have you been? I've been searching the

entire castle for you."

"I was completing my chores, as you commanded."

"Never mind that. You're coming with me."

"Now, my Lord?" Mina asked.

"Yes, now. Don't fall behind, girl. We haven't got much time."

Klodian spun around and hurried down the hall. Mina followed after him, her eyes wide with terror. She'd never seen him in such a rush. As she tried to keep up with him, she looked around for a place to leave her duster. A servant stepped out of one of the rooms and paused, bowing her head as Klodian passed her.

"Here," Mina handed her the duster, smiling at the girl's confusion.

Klodian hurried through the hallways with sure steps, never once pausing as Mina usually did. He'd designed the maze of hallways, so she wasn't surprised that he knew exactly where he was going. They exited the castle and were immediately greeted by Captain Eduard in the courtyard.

"Are the Runesmen ready?" Klodian asked.

"Yes," Eduard hesitated. "You didn't give me much time to prepare, so I'll have to use some of the recruits. Most of the seasoned men are out on patrol along the border. We're ready to follow your lead."

"Very good. I won't let this stand, no matter

what must be done."

Mina didn't understand what he was talking about, but she knew it must be important if he was taking Runesmen with him. Captain Eduard bowed and departed, heading for the barracks. Klodian continued onward and Mina spotted a carriage ahead. The horses pawed at the ground anxiously as if they were aware of Klodian's urgency.

"Get inside," Klodian ordered.

Mina looked at him in surprise, but he wasn't paying her any heed. He walked to the front of the carriage and spoke with the driver. Not wanting to lose the opportunity, Mina climbed into the carriage and sat down, marveling at the interior.

The benches were covered with plush cushions, and the walls and ceiling were elaborately decorated with velvet. Mina ran her fingertips along the soft material. Aside from everything being an ugly gold color, she found the entire experience quite amazing.

Lord Klodian stepped into the carriage and shut the door, then took a seat opposite Mina. She clasped her hands in her lap and lowered her gaze, keeping her eyes on Klodian's shoes. When the carriage didn't move, Mina cast a furtive glance at Klodian. He was staring out of the window and seemed to be waiting on something.

A few moments later, Captain Eduard's face appeared in the glass and he knocked on the carriage door twice. The carriage jerked as it began moving, and Mina sat back, trying to figure out where they might be going.

"I suppose you are curious?" Klodian asked.

"Very, my Lord."

"We're going on a hunt, but it is not like the usual trips. I'm not looking for gold and sport this time, but for blood. A dragon attacked Slia."

Mina's face scrunched in disbelief. A dragon had attacked a human settlement?

"Is that normal?" she asked.

Klodian snorted. "No, girl. I suspect it might be a young one that strayed too far from home."

"Dragons are wild animals. They aren't capable of things like retaliation, are they?" Mina didn't think so, but she envisioned the glowing eyes staring at her from the cave entrance, and she wasn't so sure.

"Of course not," Klodian replied. "But they are territorial, like any other animal. It probably left its nest and ventured far enough that it lost the scent of its fellows. It's unfortunate that it won't live long enough to learn from its mistake."

That made sense to Mina. She wondered how much damage the creature had done to Slia. She'd never been there before, but she knew the name. It was a smaller city within the Thophate Dominion, and it was the closest community to Klodian Keep.

As the time slipped away, Mina began dozing off, occasionally jolting and startling herself. Afraid that Klodian would yell at her, she tried rubbing her eyes and digging her nails into her palms, but it did little to help keep her awake. When the carriage finally stopped, she had no idea how much time had passed.

Klodian stood and stepped out of the carriage. Mina blinked repeatedly and followed after him. Now that she was moving around, she didn't feel as tired. The crunch of dirt signaled the approach of the Runesmen. Mina shielded her eyes with her right hand and saw Captain Eduard leading the small contingent of soldiers on horseback. She spotted two other familiar faces as well. Caden and Thais.

Thais.

Mina glared at her briefly before turning away. Thais was rude. And violent. Mina wanted nothing to do with the woman. She walked over to stand beside Klodian, so enwrapped in her thoughts that she didn't notice the smell of smoke in the air. She kept her eyes on the ground until a few flakes of gray ash landed at her feet. Mina realized something was wrong and lifted her head. She gasped.

Slia had been destroyed.

At least, it appeared that way to Mina. As Klodian strode forth, he motioned for her to follow him. She obeyed, gazing wide-eyed at the destruction around her. Buildings were nothing more than piles of rubble, smoke drifted into the sky in lazy plumes, and there was a terrible scent faintly masked by the smoke. Mina would later learn that it was the smell of burnt flesh.

"This is another reason why I hunt the creatures," Klodian said. "Dragons are dangerous. When they grow in numbers, their food sources become scarce. They start looking for alternatives, and that usually leads them to our cities."

"I thought you said it was a young one? If a small dragon can do this …" Mina trailed off.

"That was my assumption before we got here, but this isn't the work of one dragon. Do you sense anything?"

"No, nothing."

"I doubt the dragons have gone far. Let me know the moment you feel even the slightest hint of something."

"Yes, my Lord."

Mina winced and averted her gaze as they passed a corpse. It had been badly burned, and the lower half of it was missing entirely. She could feel bile rising in her throat, but she swallowed her saliva, forcing it back down. Klodian didn't stop moving. He continued walking through the ruined city, and it slowly became apparent to Mina that he was looking for something.

They turned left onto another street and Klodian paused. He seemed uncertain, which was out of character for him. Mina suddenly grew wary. What if the dragons were still here and she couldn't sense them? They would all be killed, and it would be her fault.

On the bright side, if she did die, at least she

would finally be free, from both Klodian's leash and her curse. Such dark thoughts used to bother her, but now … now they didn't. She didn't know if that was a good thing.

"Your ability to sense the closeness of dragons is invaluable, and not just to me. If the other Dominion Lords knew of your sixth sense, they would try to steal you from me."

Mina frowned. Why was he telling her this? Klodian grunted to himself and continued walking. Mina rubbed her leg, pressing against the scale under her pants. She didn't feel the presence of any dragons.

Klodian stopped again after a few feet. He pushed some debris around with his foot and turned to look past Mina. She glanced over her shoulder and saw Captain Eduard and the Runesmen approaching.

"This was the Dominate's house," Klodian said. "I can see his body."

"Should we search for survivors?" Eduard asked.

"Yes, but be quick. And keep your eyes open. I have a feeling the dragons that did this are still in the area."

Eduard paired the Runesmen in groups of two and sent them in various directions. Mina watched them scatter, wringing her hands anxiously. She wanted to help Klodian find the dragons responsible, but the scale wasn't giving her anything. He was probably going to be angry with her if she couldn't track them, yet what could she do?

Mina.

She whirled around at the sound of her name, but no one was there. Her eyes widened. Lord Klodian was gone.

6

So, Klodian *had* brought Mina. Caden assumed he might have, especially if the whispers of a dragon attack were true. Judging by the destruction, there was more truth to those whispers than Caden liked. After all, he hadn't signed up as a soldier to fight dragons.

"Thais and Caden, you two take the northeast side of the city. Shout if you find anything."

Caden barely heard Captain Eduard's command. He was staring at Mina. Her blonde hair seemed to shimmer in the sunlight, and she was rubbing her leg. Did she sense the dragons nearby? Fighting a man was one thing, but a dragon … he swallowed hard and tried to summon his courage.

"Come on," Thais said, pulling his arm.

They backtracked to the main street and turned left, following it east. Caden surveyed the damage as they walked. Almost all of the buildings had been decimated. The dead littered the streets, and the smell of smoke was suffocating. The heat was always rough, but with the fires still burning, it was much worse. Every so often, a slight breeze would stir, giving him the opportunity to take a fresh breath.

"I know dragons are powerful, but is this really the work of a dragon?" Thais asked. "I mean, there's nothing left."

"Lord Klodian thinks it was more than one, and I have to agree. How else would an entire city be destroyed in such a short time frame? It had to be multiple dragons."

"I suppose you're right. I just hope those beasts aren't still around."

Caden hoped so too, but he didn't say it. They reached a fork in the road. The main thoroughfare continued ahead, and a side street angled north.

"We should split up," Thais said. "We'll cover more ground that way. Besides, I don't like the feeling I get from this place."

"I don't know if that's a good idea. Captain Eduard assigned us in groups for a reason. What if something happens to you?"

Thais smirked at him. "Your concern is touching, really, but I'm a big girl. I can take care of myself."

"That's not what I meant," Caden scoffed.

"Sure you didn't. I'll take the side street. You continue ahead. If the roads don't converge at some point, we meet back here."

Caden looked back the way they'd came, unsure. "Fine," he muttered.

"See you shortly."

Thais left, and Caden watched her go. He tried not to stare, but he found it difficult. She was beautiful, he couldn't deny that, but there was something about Mina that captured more than his eyes. He barely knew the girl, true, but his attraction was more than physical. He just couldn't put his finger on it.

"Focus," he berated himself.

He continued along the main street, listening for anything other than the occasional whistle of wind through the rubble. There had to be survivors, even if there were only a few. Caden paused here and there to dig through the rubble, but all he found was death. Bodies, both burned and mutilated, were buried everywhere. The stench stung his nostrils and he vomited. He'd been in fights before and had even killed, but this was something different entirely.

Caden spat several times to clean his mouth out, then wiped his lips with the back of his hand. His throat burned, but he'd left his canteen on the saddle of his horse. It wasn't the first time he'd needed water and gone without, and it wouldn't be the last. He continued walking and tried not to breathe through his nose.

The street ended, branching off to the left and right. Stone and wood from a collapsed building blocked the way to the right, so he went left. Judging by the direction, Caden assumed he'd meet up with Thais again on this route. A scrabbling noise caught his attention, and he climbed over some rubble on the left side of the street.

He lifted a large wooden beam and shifted it aside, clearing the way into a building. He stuck his head in and looked around, but there didn't appear to be anyone inside. The sound continued, and he eventually spotted a rat. It was pinned by debris, its claws scratching as it tried to get free. Caden was about to go through the effort of saving the little thing, but then he saw the injuries it had sustained.

"Poor guy," Caden murmured.

The rat would succumb to its wounds soon, so he did the only thing he knew to do. He put the rat out of its misery by pushing down on the debris. It squealed once and was dead. Caden wiped the sweat from his brow and climbed to the top of the rubble, looking for Thais. He could see some of the other Runesmen in the distance, but there was no sign of his volatile partner.

A tingling sensation began in his neck, quickly spreading along his shoulders and down his spine. Caden looked to the sky, fearing it had something to do with a dragon. He didn't see anything other than the blinding sun. He suddenly felt weak, and his knees gave out. He slumped down face-first among the wreckage.

"Gods, what's happening to me?"

His muscles felt like jelly and refused to budge. After a few moments of panic, the realization that Lord Klodian had enacted the rune magic struck him. Was this what it would feel like all the time? He hoped not. It rendered him useless. How could he do his duty and protect the Dominion and his lord if the moment his strength was borrowed, he fell like a sack of potatoes?

As he lay there unable to move, his gaze roamed

among the hill of debris under him. Through the stones and wood, he spotted something glowing. It was small, but it blazed red as if it had been superheated. Caden kept his eyes on it, afraid that if it cooled, he'd lose sight of it. His weakness only lasted a few minutes, and then his strength came flooding back.

He hurriedly began moving the debris out of the way in an attempt to reach the glowing item. It was buried under two feet of rubble, but he managed to clear enough of it away so that he could stick his arm down through the rest to reach it. His fingers hovered around it, and despite its glow, he didn't feel any heat coming off of it.

Gritting his teeth, Caden grabbed onto it. He expected to get burned, but it was cool to the touch. He pulled his arm free and inspected the curious trinket. It had some weight to it, and he guessed it was metal. The glow faded, revealing a unique pattern of thin lines engraved on its surface.

Caden had no idea what it was, but it looked interesting. He palmed it and headed back down the mountain of ruined buildings to the street. There was still no sign of Thais, and he wondered if she'd turned back. He decided to give her a few more minutes, then he'd go searching.

While he waited, he continued to check for survivors. He didn't find any, but he did find a charred corpse and had accidentally put his hand through it when lifting a large stone. He felt his throat constrict and he gagged, but there was nothing to vomit up. He was sweaty and hot, and his patience was long gone.

"Thais!" he yelled. "Where are you?"

There was no reply. Caden growled in frustration and stormed along the street, cursing under his breath. If she had turned around …

A scream stopped him in his tracks. His best guess told him it had come from the west, and it was the scream of a woman. He sprinted toward the sound.

7

Mina screamed.

She hadn't meant to, but when Thais unexpectedly walked around the bend, it had taken her by surprise. What was she doing here? She was supposed to be looking for survivors. Mina eyed her distrustfully.

"Don't come any closer," she warned.

Thais stopped where she was, a disarming smile on her face. "Your name is Mina, right?"

Mina took a step back, her heart racing in her chest. Thais had threatened to beat her yesterday, and no one was around to stop her from acting on her words.

"Please don't run," Thais said. "I'm not going to hurt you."

"Why should I believe you?"

"It's clear that you don't. I don't blame you. Where I come from, trusting another person can get you killed. So, I won't convince you to trust me. You shouldn't. But at least hear me out."

Mina glanced over her shoulder, making note of the path she would take if she needed to flee. She looked back at Thais and tried to calm her nerves.

"What do you want to say?"

"I want to apologize. I know I can be a bit …"

Thais waved her hand as if searching for the word.

"Rude?" Mina offered.

"I was going to say brash, but that works, too."

Mina stared at Thais intently. The woman was beautiful. Her hair was long and black, woven in multiple braids that stretched past her shoulders. She wasn't much taller than Mina, but she was slightly thicker because of her sinewy form. Her eyes were a piercing blue, and they held a fire in them that seemed unquenchable. The tan hue of her skin revealed her seafaring lineage, one that was riddled with warmongering and ruthlessness before the High Prince had bent them to his will.

"Why would you apologize to me? I'm nobody."

"You are Lord Klodian's dragon finder. I hardly think that's the position of a nobody."

Thais knew nothing about her, nor about how Klodian treated her. No one did, not really. Perhaps other people didn't see her as a slave, but Mina was no fool. She knew what her role in life was, whether she liked it or not.

"While you are bound by a willing oath, I am bound against my will," Mina replied. "I am nothing more than a purchased item."

Thais shook her head. "You are more than that. Don't believe that your worth is tied to your place in life. We all have value in the eyes of Hermóðr."

Mina was surprised that Thais had apologized,

but more so that she was being nice to her. She was tempted to let her guard down, but she knew better than that. Thais was playing her for a fool. That was fine. Mina would play along. For now.

"If I forgive you, will you stop talking to me?"

"If that is what you want, then yes."

"I forgive you," Mina said.

"Good. Then we are on even ground now."

Before Mina could tell Thais to leave, Caden bounded into view. He slid to a stop, looking from Thais to Mina with a confused expression.

"What's going on?" he demanded. "I heard a scream."

"That was her," Thais said, motioning to Mina. "I startled her."

"It's true," Mina replied. "I was looking for Lord Klodian and didn't see her."

"Lord Klodian is missing?" Caden asked.

"I can't find him, but that doesn't mean he's lost. I assume he's looking for the dragons."

"They're still here?" Caden's face paled slightly.

"I don't think so," Mina answered. "I don't feel any nearby, but Lord Klodian can be … stubborn sometimes. As I said, I'm only assuming that's what he's doing."

"He used the strength rune a few moments ago," Thais said, glancing to Caden. He nodded.

"Perhaps he was lifting something heavy," Mina offered.

"Or perhaps your little ability isn't working," Thais returned. "How does it work, anyway?"

Mina felt her face flush. She didn't like attention. Thankfully, Caden diverted it elsewhere.

"We don't have time to discuss that. We need to make sure he's all right. It's our duty. Where's the last place you saw him?"

"Over there," Mina answered, pointing to where he'd been. "He was there one moment, and gone the next."

"You didn't see or hear anything?"

Mina shook her head. She didn't believe the voice she'd heard had been real, and she certainly didn't want to tell anyone about it even if it was.

Caden frowned and walked over to where Mina had pointed. He knelt and sifted the dirt around with his fingers, hobbling along the ground like some sort of crab. Mina peeked over at Thais to see if she was just as curious about his actions. The woman watched Caden with an amused smile, but there was something else in her look that told Mina that she liked him.

A pang of jealousy flashed through Mina. She wasn't sure why she felt that way. She didn't like him, not in *that* way. At least, she didn't think she did. He'd been nice to her by defending her, but that didn't mean anything … did it?

"I found his tracks," Caden said. "He went this way."

Caden stood and walked off the street, climbing over rubble and disappearing behind a crumbling building. Thais hurried after him, leaving Mina wondering if she should follow them. She decided she didn't want to be alone and ran to catch up, almost twisting her ankle attempting to balance her steps over the wreckage.

As she came around the corner of the ruined building, a strange feeling washed over her. She paused, touching the scale on her leg. The sensation was different from what she normally felt when a dragon was near, but it was definitely coming from the scale.

Caden was searching ahead, but Thais had gone a different route. Mina watched them as she tried to get her bearings, but a wave of nausea caused her to double over. She clutched her stomach and gritted her teeth, curling into a ball on the ground. Her mouth opened, but nothing came out except a gasp of air.

"Help," she managed to say, but it was barely above a whisper.

The air in front of her seemed to ripple like the surface of a pond disturbed by something. She fought against the ill feeling and stretched her hand toward it. Her nausea intensified and she recoiled, screaming within her mind as tears escaped her eyes.

Gods, make it go away!

Mina lay there tremoring, holding herself. Eventually, the sensation faded, leaving her feeling weak and tired. Once her strength returned, she sat up and brushed her hair out of her eyes. The air was no longer rippling. She touched her leg. Nothing was coming from the scale. Had that been the presence of a dragon? If so, it must have been powerful indeed to have such an effect on her.

Fear coursed through her. If that had been a dragon, then Klodian might be dead. Mina scrambled to her feet, leaning against the rubble momentarily. She needed to find him. If he had been killed, then her curse would never be lifted.

"Over here!" Caden shouted. "I found him!"

8

Caden knelt beside Lord Klodian's prone form.

His chest moved up and down with his breathing, and Caden heaved a sigh of relief. At first, he'd feared his lord was dead. A glance at their surroundings didn't reveal much. Everything was a mass of rubble like the rest of the city, and there were no signs that anything foul had caused Klodian to fall unconscious.

Still, the man wasn't lying on the ground for no reason. Caden kept his hand on the hilt of his sword just in case, though he didn't know what he would be able to do against a dragon. Thais joined him first. Her eyes widened in surprise.

"He's alive, but I'm not sure what happened. I found him here like this."

"If a dragon attacked him, there'd be nothing left," Thais said.

"My thoughts exactly. That doesn't mean we're clear of danger, though. Go find Captain Eduard. We need to get Lord Klodian to safety."

"I don't like being told what to do, but I'll make an exception this time. Next time I better hear the word 'please.'"

Thais flashed him a grin and rushed off. A moment later, Mina cautiously approached. Her face was pale and she looked like she might faint.

"Is he …"

"No, he's fine. For now, at least. Thais went to get help. Are you all right? You look sick."

"It's nothing," Mina replied.

It was obvious she was lying, but Caden decided not to press her. He nodded instead and lifted the visor of Klodian's helm. His eyelids were open, but only the whites of his eyes were showing. Caden gently pulled the helm off completely and set it aside.

"Has he ever gone unconscious before? Maybe when he uses the rune magic?"

"No, never."

Mina seemed nervous, which confused him. He wondered why she was so concerned about Klodian. If he died, she would no longer be a slave. She would also no longer have a home, but to Caden, freedom seemed more important than things like food and shelter. Mina swayed on her feet, and she blinked lazily.

"You should probably sit down," Caden said. "You don't look so good."

"I'm fine. Just focus on Lord Klodian."

They both went silent. The time ticked along, seeming to last indefinitely until the sound of several people approaching broke the stillness. Thais had returned, leading Captain Eduard and a few other Runesmen.

"What happened?" Eduard demanded.

"I'm not sure. He was already down when I found him."

Eduard motioned to the other Runesmen. "Find something stable to put him on. We'll carry him out of here and have the physicians look at him back at the castle."

In short order, a thin flat piece of wood was brought over and they lifted Lord Klodian and placed him onto it, using the board as a makeshift stretcher. Eduard ordered everyone to grab a side, and together, they raised it off the ground and started navigating slowly over the rubble. Caden glanced over his shoulder at Mina.

She followed them, but she seemed to be struggling. Caden was forced to keep his main focus on Klodian, namely keeping his end of the board up high enough without tripping, but he continually checked on Mina when there was a pause.

As they made it onto the street, Caden heard a groan and looked back just in time to see Mina stumble and fall. She hit the ground hard and didn't move.

"Captain! The girl!"

Eduard called a halt and walked over to her, but he made no move to help her. He stood over her in silence for a moment, then turned to look at Caden.

"We can come back for her."

Caden scrunched his face. "Sir?"

"Lord Klodian's well-being is more important

than hers. After we've tended to him, we can worry about her."

"I'm sorry sir, but I don't think Lord Klodian would approve." Eduard gave him a hard stare. "She's the key to his wealth. If we left her out here, I'd hate to see the punishment he'd inflict on the one responsible."

Caden caught a slight change in Eduard's demeanor. It was subtle, but it was there.

"Good point, Runesman. You can carry her."

Eduard strode past Caden and ordered the others to continue. Caden hoped he hadn't overstepped a line with the captain, but he couldn't in good conscience leave someone to die. And he knew he wasn't wrong. If Klodian found out they'd intentionally left Mina, he would probably lash the entire lot of them.

Caden lifted Mina in his arms and slung her over his shoulder, then hurried to catch up with the others. They trudged through the ruined city back to where the carriage and their mounts waited. The desert was always a quiet place, but Caden found the stillness of Slia to be eerie.

He reached the carriage just as Lord Klodian had been placed inside. Captain Eduard offered him a nod as he stepped out, which led Caden to believe he hadn't completely messed up.

"Put the girl in there and ride along with them. I can't be in two places at once, so keep your eyes on Lord Klodian. If anything happens, knock twice on the front wall. The driver will stop and I'll know there's a problem."

Caden wasn't sure if his assignment was a punishment or a reward. He didn't mind riding in the cool shade, but he also didn't want the other Runesmen to think he'd been elevated above them without merit. Perhaps he was overthinking things, but he knew how petty people could be.

"Yes, sir."

Eduard waited until Caden had entered the carriage, then he closed the door and began shouting orders. Lord Klodian was lying on one side of the carriage, stretched out across the pillowed bench. Caden placed Mina on the other side, in the same position, and stood in the center. The carriage started moving and he held onto the wall for support.

His gaze flicked back and forth between Lord Klodian and Mina, making sure they were breathing normally. Aside from being unconscious, Lord Klodian didn't seem to have sustained any wounds. It was a mystery, but one that would hopefully be solved by the physicians. After a long while, Mina's eyes fluttered open.

"How are you feeling?" he asked.

She watched him with a thoughtful expression on her face and slowly sat up, hugging her knees to her chest.

"I feel better," she replied.

"You scared me back there. I'm glad you're all

right."

Mina's cheeks blushed, but she didn't say anything. They rode in silence, both of them watching over Lord Klodian. Eventually, Mina released her legs and let them hang down off the bench. That's when Caden spotted a glint of copper. She must have torn her pants when she'd fallen. Mina followed his gaze and her eyes widened. She tried to cover the scale with her hands, cursing lowly.

"I'm not bothered by it," Caden said.

"Maybe not, but I am. I hate this cursed thing."

"Some would see it as a blessing rather than a curse."

"And such people would be wrong," Mina retorted. "No one knows what it's like to feel the presence of those creatures in their mind. I wouldn't wish it on my worst enemies."

As he listened to her, Caden wondered if he would have the fortitude to deal with something like that. It was unheard of. A human who could sense dragons. He'd heard the things whispered about her. Some called her a witch, others a demon spawn. They were all wrong, he knew. She was just different, and people had trouble understanding that.

"Were you born in Klodan's court?" Caden asked.

"No. My parents sold me to him when I was young."

"They *sold* you? Isn't that illegal?"

Mina snorted. "Many things are illegal, but that doesn't stop anyone."

"I know that, it's just … your own family sold you. I can't believe anyone would do that."

"I blame this stupid scale. And the dragon that it belongs to. That's why I help him, you know."

"Why?"

"To rid the world of the beasts. Dragons are mindless animals, good for nothing other than their treasure troves. Lord Klodian grows richer, and I get a little bit of revenge with each one that is killed."

Caden was surprised at how much hatred she harbored. She seemed like such a meek woman, and yet as she spoke, he could hear the unbridled rage burning within her voice. She didn't just dislike dragons, she despised them.

"How did it happen?" Caden asked.

Mina stared at him, and he assumed he'd offended her. He was about to apologize when she answered.

"I fell into the nest of a dragon. While I was playing in the hills, I stepped on a weak spot and it collapsed. The nest was abandoned, thank the gods, but they had left a great pile of discarded scales. I landed on it and this was my reward."

She removed her hands from her leg and Caden got a better look at it. It was a deep copper color and pentagonal in shape. The two sides were longer, while the top and bottom edges were shorter in diameter. It was curved flush with her thigh, which Caden found intriguing. He'd assumed the scale would be protruding out of her, but given that she wore normal clothes, he realized that was a foolish assumption.

"Did your parents try to remove it?"

"They did. And so too did the local physicians. The scale fused into my flesh somehow and … became a part of me. My parents were told that the only option was to remove my leg. They probably would have gone through with that option had it not been for the other thing."

"What do you mean?"

"The ability to sense dragons. I didn't know that's what it was until I followed the pull. I led my parents to a den of dragons and almost got us all killed. I think that's when they realized that I wasn't just deformed. I was cursed. Lord Klodian heard the rumors about me and my parents sold me to him. There's not much else to tell."

Caden sat down on the bench beside her and tried to fathom how parents could sell their own flesh and blood. By the time they returned to the castle, he still didn't have an answer.

9

Mina's strength didn't fully return until evening fell.

The chaos that had engulfed the castle had finally died down, though the servants talked about the steady stream of physicians still coming and going from Lord Klodian's chambers. Mina had spent the remainder of the day in her bed, but she hadn't been able to sleep. She didn't have the energy to finish her chores, and she doubted anyone would notice they weren't done.

Lord Klodian would, but since he was still unconscious, she wasn't afraid of earning his wrath. Left to her own devices for the first time in a while, her mind replayed the events at Slia over and over again. The odd sensation she'd felt still troubled her. It had definitely originated from the scale, but it didn't feel like any dragon she'd sensed before.

"How are you feeling?" Vhan's voice broke her reverie and she rolled over to look at him.

"Better," she replied.

"That's good."

"What of Lord Klodian?"

"Nothing to report yet. The physicians all seem stumped. He hasn't suffered any visible wounds, but they can't explain why he hasn't awakened yet. Despite that, they seem to agree that he should be all right. They're saying it might take some time for him to come out of whatever state he's in."

Mina wasn't sure those old men knew what they were talking about. If there were no wounds and he hadn't awakened yet, something was wrong. There was nothing she could do about it, though, so she tried not to think about what would happen if Klodian died.

"Are you hungry?" Vhan changed the subject. "Dinner is almost ready. If you don't think you can make it to the dining hall, I can bring you something."

"I appreciate the offer, but I think I can manage," Mina said.

She was hungry, and she felt like herself again, so she sat up and slipped her ragged shoes on. She was waiting until she had enough money to buy a new pair of sturdy boots, but since Klodian didn't pay her, it was taking a long time to scrape the coins together.

"I wouldn't mind some company if you don't have anything else to do."

Vhan smiled. "I've got the night off, believe it or not."

"So do I. It's kind of odd, isn't it?"

"It really is," Vhan agreed. "I almost don't know what to do with myself."

Mina laughed, which wasn't something she did often. It felt good to feel unburdened, even if it wouldn't last long.

"Come on, I'm famished."

Vhan walked beside her as they navigated the maze of halls, and they reached the dining hall to find that the Runesmen were being served. Mina usually didn't eat until later in the evening, so she was surprised to see so many people in the hall at one time. Caden and Thais were there too, talking amongst themselves at the end of one of the long tables.

Mina and Vhan joined the line of people waiting to be served, eventually getting a plate full of steaming chicken smothered in a cheese sauce and a bowl of broth. The food at Klodian Keep was the only thing that Mina had never complained about. Lord Klodian didn't scrimp when it came to nourishing his soldiers and staff, and although Mina was a slave, he didn't exclude her.

She followed Vhan to an empty section of one of the tables and they ate in silence. The room, however, wasn't quiet. The Runesmen were a rowdy bunch. Bits and pieces of loud conversations reached Mina's ears, and she heard everything from stories about where people were from to the destruction of Slia. The loudness was a little overwhelming, and after she finished her meal, she rose to her feet.

"Thank you for eating with me," she said to Vhan. "I should probably get some rest."

"You're welcome," he grinned at her like a fool. "Does this mean you'll let me see the scale?"

Mina rolled her eyes at him. "No."

"It was worth a try," he said with a chuckle, then shrugged. "Just leave your plate and bowl here. The kitchen staff will collect them."

"Are you sure?"

"Yes. It's their job, you know."

"Oh, right. Well, good night, Vhan. I'll see you tomorrow."

"See you tomorrow."

Mina left the noisy dining hall and returned to her bed. With her stomach full, it didn't take her long to fall asleep. Her dreams didn't let her rest, and she tossed and turned from continuous nightmares. She felt as if she had just fallen back to sleep when someone touched her shoulder.

She opened her eyes to see Captain Eduard. He pressed his finger to his lips and motioned to the hall. Mina got up and followed him, wondering why he was summoning her. Her heart began racing in her chest. Once they were out of the room, Eduard spoke lowly.

"Lord Klodian wants to see you."

"He's awake?"

"Yes, but he's very weak. I told him it could wait until morning, but he demanded I come and get you."

"Is he going to be all right?"

"He'll be fine. Let's go. I'd like to get *some*

sleep tonight."

Captain Eduard escorted her to Lord Klodian's bedchamber. At the door, he stopped and nodded for her to enter. She pushed the door open and stepped inside. Eduard shut it behind her, and she heard his receding footsteps echo down the hall as he left.

The room was mostly dark, but a few candles were lit, their flames burning steady. She walked further into the room and paused when she saw Lord Klodian. He was sitting up in his bed, his back against the headboard. A mound of pillows surrounded him. Mina paused. He appeared to be sleeping. She was about to turn around when he spoke.

"Sit, girl."

His voice was little more than a rasp. In the dimly lit room, it was almost creepy. Mina stepped toward a chair against the wall, and Klodian hissed in disapproval.

"Over here. On the floor."

She obeyed, sitting on the plush rug that covered the cold stones, gritting her teeth while doing it. Mina hated that he treated her like a dog. She was relieved to see that he was alive, but that didn't mean she cared about him. She only wanted her freedom, and unfortunately, he was the only key to that door.

"Did you sense a dragon at Slia today?"

"No, my Lord." She hesitated. "I … don't think

I did."

"Interesting. Explain yourself."

"It's difficult to describe, but when I sense a dragon, it's very distinct. I just know that's what it is. Today I felt something, but it wasn't the same. It was ... different, odd. I don't know what it was, but it made me sick."

Lord Klodian was silent for a long while, and Mina wondered if he'd fallen asleep. He stirred, reaching up to lazily scratch his cheek. She had never seen him so vulnerable before. The thought of killing him flitted through her mind, but she discounted it almost immediately. She wasn't a murderer, no matter how much she thought he might deserve it. And as much as she hated to admit it, she needed Klodian.

"I think you might have felt the touch of magic," he said.

"My Lord?"

"I didn't stutter, girl. Something, or someone, attacked me out there. I didn't see anyone, but it's the only explanation I have."

"Why do you think I felt magic? Only Runesmen can feel it when their lord uses it unless I am mistaken?"

Lord Klodian turned his head toward her.

"There are other forms of magic in the world. Even you have surely heard the rumors."

"I have, my Lord, but they are only that: rumors.

The High Prince outlawed everything except rune magic."

Klodian laughed weakly, but there was no joy in it.

"The High Prince has outlawed many things, but people always find ways around the rule of law. There are rogues out there who practice banned magic. They are called mages. Their powers are far different from rune magic, and much more dangerous. I think one of them attacked me, though I have yet to figure out why. Perhaps it was another assassination attempt or a survivor from the dragon attack. Either way, I believe that scale can alert you to the presence of magic."

Mina didn't want to believe it, but it made sense. The sensation was too different to have been a dragon. There was no explanation to her aversion to it, though. It had made her physically ill, enough that she'd been useless.

"That might be true, though I desperately hope it is not."

"Of course you don't," Klodian said. "You already see your dragon sense as a curse. If you can also sense magic, I'm sure you'll hate that scale even more."

"You know me too well, my Lord."

"Not well enough, it would seem. How this evaded my notice is beyond me. Unless you knew and hid it from me?"

Although his words were weak and hoarse, the

veiled threat behind his question sent a shiver along Mina's spine.

"It is as new to me as it is to you. I would not hide something like that, my Lord."

Klodian nodded slowly. "I believe you. As soon as my strength returns, we are going to put your new power to the test." He breathed heavily for a moment. "Leave me. I need to rest."

As Mina made her way back to the servant's chamber, a bad feeling was worming its way into her stomach.

10

After dinner, Caden and the other Runesmen retired to the barracks. Darkness had fallen, and there was still no word from anyone on Lord Klodian's status. Caden shuffled along behind his fellow soldiers, Thais beside him.

His thoughts kept returning to the odd thing he'd found in Slia. He'd stashed it in the upper portion of his right boot to keep from losing it, and it had eventually worked its way down until he was walking on it. It pressed painfully against the sole of his foot, but he ignored the ache and listened to Thais as she talked.

"What happens if Lord Klodian never wakes up?" she asked.

"Don't say things like that," Caden replied, glaring at her.

"Why not? Everyone's thinking it. I'm just saying it. And it's a valid question. Who takes his position if he dies?"

"How would I know? I'm a lowly peon like you. But if I had to guess, I'd say the High Prince would appoint someone else. Lord Klodian isn't married and he has no children, so there's no heir to his title."

"That's a fair assumption. I figured the next in command would be promoted, but I suppose being a Dominion Lord doesn't fall into the same line of power."

"There's something I want to show you," Caden said, lowering his voice.

"What is it?"

"Meet me at my bed once the lights go out."

Thais side-eyed him, and a flirtatious grin was pulling at her lips. Realizing that his words sounded like he was talking about something else, he laughed and shook his head.

"It's nothing like that."

"Right. I've fallen for that a time or two, but not anymore."

"I'm serious. I found something in Slia, but I don't know what it is."

"If you say so. If I find you with your clothes off ..." Thais didn't finish her sentence. Caden wondered if she'd actually be mad if he did that, then quickly pushed the thought aside. He would never do something so crass. Well, maybe if he were drunk, but certainly not if he was in his right mind.

The Runesmen filed into the barracks and dispersed to their designated spots. Caden sat on his cot and pulled his boots off with a grunt, thankful to be off his feet. Despite no one seeing an enemy, dragon or otherwise, Captain Eduard had placed the castle on high alert. Lord Klodian's mysterious circumstances had everyone speculating, and all of the soldiers at the castle had been forced into taking shifts at watch.

As the day went on and nothing happened, Eduard had relaxed the shifts to allow for dinner and rest. Caden was as bothered about things as much as everyone else, but there was no use in fretting about it. Some things were outside of his control. The key was learning to accept that.

He tilted his right boot upside down and caught the metal piece as it fell out, then laid down and turned the item over in his hands. Now that it wasn't glowing at all, he could see that it was a silvery gray hue. The unique pattern of lines was still visible, too. Caden ran a finger over the ridges. They were smooth. The entire piece was smooth, aside from one jagged edge that appeared to be a break line. Whatever the thing was, it had broken off of something.

Once the lanterns were extinguished and snoring filled the air, Thais approached his cot. The room was slightly illuminated from the moonlight that filtered through the windows, and he could see that she was regarding him with a thoughtful look.

"What?" Caden asked.

"You surprised me."

"How so?"

"I expected to find you naked. I thought you were joking about finding something."

"Are you disappointed that I'm not?" Caden had his suspicions that she was attracted to him, but he wanted to be certain before he tried to pursue anything with her. It was funny how quickly he'd changed his mind about her.

"Don't worry about that. What do you want to show me?"

"This."

He held the item up so that a shaft of light caught it. Thais reached for it, and Caden pulled his hand away.

"I'm not going to steal it from you," she huffed. "I just want to see it closer."

He handed it to her, and she peered closely at it. Her left brow rose, and she turned her eyes on him.

"You found this in Slia?"

"Yes. It was buried under some debris, and it was glowing red when I first saw it, but it wasn't hot."

"Don't you know what this is?" she asked.

"Should I?"

"It's a piece of irite."

Caden stared at her blankly, shaking his head slightly. "What's that?"

"It's a type of metal, but it is only found in one place that I know of, and it isn't anywhere near here."

"Maybe someone in Slia imported it. What's the big deal?"

"Nothing really, other than it grows on a

creature that lives on a volcanic mountain. It's basically a giant snail that makes its home in the vents of the volcano. The irite acts as a shield from the heat. It's an interesting creature, but they're harmless. I think it's odd you found this in Slia, given that it was attacked by a dragon."

"Why is that odd? You said it's basically a piece of a snail."

"Yes, but it's heat resistant. What do you think burns hotter, dragon fire or a volcano?"

"Probably a volcano, but what do I know?"

"Not much, apparently," Thais quipped with a grin. "You guessed right, though. People have been trying to use irite for years, but no one has figured out how. It's sort of like iron, but it has different properties. It's almost impossible to shape it."

"You seem to know a lot about it," Caden said.

Thais shrugged. "My father spent some time around merchants that had a plan to sell the stuff, but no one wanted it. I had the misfortune of having to listen to their entire conversation on the matter."

"Was your father a merchant?"

"No. He was a soldier."

"A Runesman?"

"No, he was a leader. A commander. He died in battle a few years ago."

"Did he serve Lord Klodian?" Caden was surprised that Thais was openly sharing so much with him.

"I wish he had. He served in another Dominion under Lord Culver. The man is a tyrant. When my father died, Lord Culver called him a failure and banished me and my mother from his Dominion. We came to the Thophate because no one wanted to risk Lord Culver's anger."

"Lord Klodian didn't care, huh?"

"Lord Klodian doesn't know," Thais clarified. "I shouldn't have told you that."

"Don't worry, I won't say anything," Caden replied. "What is there to gain by bringing you trouble?"

"Nothing besides a pummeling."

"What about your mother? Did you join the Runesmen to help her with money?"

"She's dead, too." Thais's expression darkened. "I'm tired of talking about this stuff."

"I didn't intend to pry into your history. I'm sorry."

"It's fine. I'm going to bed. It's been a long day."

Caden half-expected Thais to climb onto his cot again, but instead, she handed him the irite piece and went to her own bed. He put the irite under his pillow and considered her words. Was it possible someone had figured out how to use the metal? And if so, what were they doing with it?

11

It was still dark when one of the servants woke Mina.

She rolled over, bleary-eyed, and tried to focus on the girl's face. It was Kera. Or Fera. She wasn't sure, as it was hard to tell the twins apart.

"Lord Klodian has asked for you," the girl whispered.

"It's still dark," Mina groaned. "What could he possibly want at this hour?"

"Dawn is on the horizon. And you know how he can be, so please don't fall back asleep."

The girl crept back to her own bed and climbed in, pulling the blanket over her head. Mina yawned and laid there for a moment, trying to force herself into wakefulness. She felt as if she'd only just fallen asleep, and it didn't help that he'd also woken her in the middle of the night. She forced herself out of bed and sluggishly put her worn shoes on, then made her way into the hall.

Lord Klodian was waiting for her, along with two other men. They were all dressed in plain clothes, which made Mina pause. She'd never seen Klodian dressed down before. It was a peculiar sight.

"My Lord?"

Klodian looked her over. "You'll fit in as you

are," he said. "Come, the carriage is waiting for us."

"Carriage? What's going on?"

"I told you, we're going to test your new skill. And I know just the place."

Mina stared at Klodian, trying to wrap her tired mind around his words. Just hours ago, he'd looked frail and tired. And now he appeared to be back to his usual self. There was no rasp to his voice or anything. It occurred to her that he was probably using his rune magic.

"We're leaving now, my Lord?"

"Yes. We're going to be traveling a fair distance, and I want to be back by nightfall."

"Where are we going?" Mina asked.

"To the borderlands, near the Phalan Dominion. Your questions are wasting time. Let's go."

Klodian turned on his heel and started walking. One of the guards followed beside him, and the other waited for Mina. She rubbed the sleep from her eyes and sighed. If the cursed scale offered her another ability, she was going to rip it out of her flesh, no matter the pain.

The four of them entered the carriage and they were off, heading north toward the border. Mina was curious as to why Klodian was dressed as a commoner, but she was more curious as to why he'd only brought two guards with him. She'd heard that the cities located along the borders of the Dominions were dangerous places, filled with people who didn't respect the laws of either Dominion. If that were true, Mina suspected that Lord Klodian was sorely understaffed.

The journey took several hours, and the trip was uneventful. Mina was surprised she stayed awake the entire time, especially considering she hadn't gotten much sleep. She kept her gaze out the window or on the floor, trying her best to avoid looking at Klodian or his men. Eventually, she spotted a sprawling metropolitan that resembled an oversized camp more than it did a city. There was no wall surrounding it, and the place was teeming with people of all cultures swarming in and out of large multicolored tents.

Once the carriage stopped, the two guards exited and surveyed the area, then motioned for Lord Klodian. He stepped out into the open and looked over his shoulder at Mina.

"This should be the ideal place for you to sense magic. Karapen is the busiest city on the border, and there are people from many other Dominions. If someone is using outlawed magic, this is where they will be."

Mina stood and subconsciously rubbed the scale on her leg. She didn't feel anything yet, but if sensing magic was the same as sensing dragons, she'd have to be within a few hundred feet of the person. Her stomach rumbled, though she wasn't entirely sure if it was from hunger. She was anxious, and sweat was collecting on her palms.

I just want to get this over with, she thought as

she slowly stepped down the carriage steps. She noticed that the heat wasn't as bad. It was still hot, but there was a heaviness to the air that she wasn't accustomed to. She glanced at Lord Klodian, wondering again why he was dressed down.

"Don't speak to anyone," Klodian said. "And don't wander off. We'll travel together at all times. If you see something suspicious, say something. I may be perceptive, but I can't be aware of every danger. My runes aren't as strong at this distance, and I'd rather avoid trouble if we can."

"Yes, my Lord."

Klodian looked at her. "Call me Ardit," he said. "I don't need anyone realizing I'm a Dominion Lord, or they'll all be petitioning their needs and wants at my feet."

"As you say, my L—" Mina paused. "Ardit."

Ardit was his first name, but Mina had never heard anyone call him by it. He was always addressed properly with his title, so it would take her some time to get accustomed to using anything else. Klodian motioned to the city.

"Karapen has a district where magical items are sold, charms and such. We'll start there and work our way through the city. With any luck, we'll determine your skill quickly and be on our way. I'm not fond of these clothes, and I don't like being this far from home without an army."

"I will do my best," Mina said.

Klodian took the lead, his two guards flanking

him on either side. Mina walked behind them, gazing wide-eyed at all the foreign sights. They passed tents of all sizes and colors, and the goods being sold within them ranged from weapons and armor to bright rugs and ornate tapestries.

A few of the vendors called out to her in the common tongue, but many of them spoke in languages she'd never heard before. They continued along the main road, which was comprised of well-trampled dirt that had been packed down from use. Side streets veered off in various directions, but Klodian kept them going straight until they reached a large intersection. He led them to the left, and Mina noticed there was considerably less foot traffic.

She immediately realized why.

The tents and stalls on this street were for people looking for magical items. Potions, charms, and spellbooks were everywhere, and the people selling them were just as fascinating. Some of the vendors had strange markings inked into their flesh, while others had a variety of piercings on their faces. Despite their appearances, Mina didn't feel afraid. She was more intrigued than anything, with a host of questions forming in her mind.

"Do you sense anything?" Klodian asked lowly, looking back at her.

Mina shook her head. The scale wasn't doing anything, and she didn't feel ill or nauseous. As they traveled further down the street, the items being sold became abundantly stranger. Dead animals, talismans made of bones and teeth, and many other things that Mina didn't recognize. A feeling of darkness settled over her, and she glanced around fearfully.

"My Lo—er, Ardit?"

"Yes, girl?"

"I don't like this place. It feels … bad."

"I imagine so. These people practice shadow magic. It's banned like the other types, but shadow magic is especially dangerous. To use it, the caster must take life from something to work their spells."

"They kill people?"

"Yes, and animals. They are a wicked lot."

Mina could feel the darkness closing in around her, a heavy weight that tried to suffocate her. She swallowed hard and kept close to Klodian and his guards, but that didn't make her feel any safer. Her heart began to race, and …

Her eyes shot to the right. She could sense something, but it wasn't the odd sensation she'd felt in Slia. No, this was a familiar feeling, one she knew all too well. She focused on the pull. It was on the other side of the tents, close, but not too powerful. It had to be a young one, younger than any she'd felt before.

Mina pushed past the guards and took the lead. Klodian didn't question her. He just followed; his steps quickening to keep pace with her. The pull was guiding her to the right, but she couldn't see anything with all of the tents in the way. She hurried to the end of the street and turned the corner. A massive green and yellow tent caught her attention.

That was it.

She checked to make sure Klodian and the guards were still with her, and Klodian nodded at her. He placed his hand on the hilt of his sword, and the guards did the same. Mina turned back to the tent. While it was enormous, it didn't seem big enough to house a dragon. It had to be young indeed if it could fit inside that space. Mina paused at the entrance, her heart pounding in her ears.

"What is it, girl? Dragon or magic?"

Mina grabbed onto the tent flap and pulled it open.

12

When the morning horn blared, Caden was already awake and prepared.

He was one of the first to rush out of the barracks and begin the morning run around the castle. Captain Eduard had told them ten laps. That had seemed easy enough, but as yesterday had proved, it was much more difficult than he first thought. Midway through his second lap, he could feel the soreness in his muscles flaring to life.

He kept a smooth pace and tried to focus on something other than the pain. His thoughts turned to Lord Klodian, and he wondered how the man was faring. Klodian seemed tough, and Caden had heard the stories about how he had evaded multiple assassination attempts. Whatever had happened to him yesterday in Slia, it hardly seemed possible to keep him down for long.

The morning air was crisp and cool. Within a few hours, the sun would start baking the land with its unforgivable heat. For now, Caden enjoyed the slight chill. He was well ahead of his fellow Runesmen, by at least two laps, but it wasn't a competition. It was about endurance and training his body. By the time he finished his final lap, the sun had driven the chill away.

Caden entered the castle for breakfast. The line was nonexistent, and he got fresh servings of scrambled eggs, two biscuits smothered in gravy, and a thick slice of ham. The steaming food made his mouth water and he devoured the meal hungrily. The other Runesmen began to file into the dining hall, and Thais carried her tray to where he was, sitting down beside him.

"You trying to show off or something?" she asked.

"No, why?"

"Just asking. You didn't wait for anyone before you bolted off like a dog on the scent of its prey."

Caden smiled. "I just love to start my days with a relaxing run, so I was eager to get going."

Thais eyed him like he was insane before his sarcasm dawned on her. She rolled her eyes and shook her head.

"Oh, we've got a jester here. Great."

"I'll be here all week," Caden said.

"You'll be here longer than that, I hope. You don't plan on dying anytime soon, do you?"

"No, of course not."

Caden considered telling her his plan, but he decided to keep his mouth shut. He'd initially assumed his days of training would be torture and that he would end up keeping to himself, a lone wolf among the pack. It was only his second full day as a Runesman and he felt more at home than he had in a long time.

It was a great feeling, but if he wanted to make a

name for himself, he would still need to transfer Dominions. He was feeling conflicted, which made things confusing. Should he stay where he was and be content with the way things were, or should he forge ahead with his plan?

He didn't know the answer. Not yet.

Thais dug into her food, but she turned to him and spoke with her mouth full.

"You should show Captain Eduard what you found in Slia."

Caden's face scrunched in confusion. "Why?"

"The more I think about it, the more I'm convinced there's something strange going on. Supposedly, multiple dragons attacked and there was no sign of them when we got there."

"What does that have to do with the irite? And besides that, the attack was a couple of hours before we arrived. That's plenty of time for the creatures to flee."

"Weren't you listening to me last night? Irite is heat resistant."

"And?"

Thais was about to shovel more food into her mouth, but paused and stared incredulously at Caden.

"You're really not putting these things together? If someone could craft a shield or some kind of armor that was resistant to dragon fire, what do you think they would do with that? Slay dragons easier?

Sure, maybe someone like Lord Klodian would do that. But someone like Lord Culver would think bigger, with greed as their driving force. Someone like Lord Culver would find a way to utilize irite to their advantage and force dragons to do their bidding."

Caden was silent for a long moment. Thais continued eating as if she hadn't just made a wild leap in logic, which worried him. She wasn't serious, was she?

"You think that someone orchestrated that attack on Slia? Someone who has a way of controlling dragons?"

"Yes."

"You can't be serious," Caden said, laughing nervously. "That's outlandish thinking. And it's impossible."

"How do you know it's impossible?" Thais asked.

"It's never happened before. If it was possible, I'm sure someone would have figured it out by now and we'd be waging battle from dragon back. Think about it, Thais. Really imagine that in your mind. Someone controlling a dragon?" He snorted. "I think you've been hit in the head one too many times."

"You don't have to believe what I do, but don't mock me for it. We might be friends now, but I'll still slap the fire out of your backside."

"I'm sorry, I didn't mean to offend you. It's just

… you don't really believe that, do you?"

Thais shrugged. "So what if I do? Are you going to call me crazy next? Hurl insults all you want. I can take it. I've got thicker skin than you know. But mark my words: if I'm right and something bad happens, it's all on you. I'm just saying that you should tell Captain Eduard what you found. I'll tell him what I think is happening, and if he laughs us off, then the blame is on him. If he doesn't and I turn out to be right, then we'll be heroes."

Caden couldn't believe what she was saying. There was absolutely no way he was going to tell anyone her conspiracy theory, especially not Captain Eduard. They'd both be kicked out of the Runesmen for mental instability.

"If that's what you believe, more power to you, but I'm not having any part of it. And there's no blame to be cast at me even if you are right. I found a piece of metal, nothing more. I'll see you on the field."

Caden left the dining hall and departed the castle, turning toward the practice field. The idea that someone was controlling dragons for some nefarious purpose was absurd. If he didn't know any better, and he might not, he'd say Thais *was* crazy. Maybe she was stressed. She had brought up has past last night, and those were some deep emotional wounds. The death of a parent could have that effect on anyone.

He waited for the other Runesmen so they could begin their training. Captain Eduard was the first one to join him on the field, and he offered an impressed nod to Caden.

"You did well yesterday," Eduard said. "Finding Lord Klodian like that must have been frightening."

"A little," Caden admitted. "I thought he was dead at first. Is he all right? We haven't heard anything about him."

"He's fine. He left this morning for personal business, but he'll be back tonight."

Caden felt a wave of relief wash over him. "Thank the gods. What happened to him?"

Eduard shook his head. "No one knows. He awoke in the middle of the night, weak and confused. The physicians didn't find any wounds. No poison was in his system, nothing. It's a conundrum."

"I imagine so. I'm glad he's all right."

Loud voices filled the air as the other Runesmen began to approach the field. Eduard stepped close to Caden and lowered his voice.

"You might think you've gotten away with it, but I've got my eyes on you."

"Sir?" Caden asked, confused.

"It's quite a coincidence that he was alone when you found him. He doesn't remember much, and the slave girl said he disappeared before she knew he was gone. It all sounds suspicious to me. An inside job done by a traitor. Possibly two. What would you know about that?"

"Nothing, sir. I told you everything I know."

"We'll see about that. If you're lying to me, I'll find out." Eduard turned toward the other Runesmen. "Line up!" he shouted. "Today you'll be sparring!"

Caden stared at the captain. Did he think that Caden had done something to Lord Klodian? That was more absurd than Thais's theory. As if summoned by his thoughts, Thais marched over to stand beside him in the line, a scowl on her face. He closed his eyes and sighed.

Not only was Thais upset with him, but Eduard also suspected him of a crime he didn't commit. Maybe transferring to another Dominion wasn't a bad idea after all.

13

"Welcome! Come in, come in!"

The jovial voice came from a tall dark-skinned man standing near the center of the tent. He grinned broadly and motioned for Mina to enter. She glanced around the tent and spotted the source of the pull. It *was* a dragon, but it was the smallest one she'd ever seen. It was curled up on a rug, but it snapped its brass-colored head up and gazed at her as she stepped inside.

Lord Klodian and one of the guards followed her, and she guessed the other one was standing watch outside. Klodian looked at the dragon first, then to the merchant. Mina was confused. The dark-skinned man didn't appear to be afraid of the beast. It was roughly the size of a horse, but still … it was a dragon.

"You come looking for spices, yes? I have many to choose from."

The man motioned to the racks around the tent. The shelves were filled with glass jars containing a variety of colored spices.

"Yes, we're here for spice," Lord Klodian answered. "Gareth, find me some cinnamon, would you?"

"There should be some cinnamon on the rack there," the merchant said, pointing to the rack along the far-right wall.

Klodian nodded toward the dragon. "I've never seen one like it before."

"Ah, yes. Draak isn't from this Dominion. I brought him from across the border."

"You gave it a name?" Klodian seemed appalled.

"Yes. He is my pet. Do you not name your pets, good sir?"

"Yes, but dragons are not pets. In my Dominion, we kill dragons. They are mindless creatures that cause nothing but destruction."

Mina was listening to their exchange, but she was also watching the dragon curiously. It returned her stare, sniffing at the air.

"Dragons are smarter than people realize," the merchant said. "This one can even do tricks. Draak, come here."

The dragon ignored him and continued to gaze at Mina. The merchant snapped his fingers a few times, but it didn't do any good.

"Bah! They can be stubborn things when they want."

Mina tore her eyes away from the dragon and looked at Klodian.

"How much for the cinnamon?" he asked as the guard came back holding a jar.

"Two silver, no minted images on them. I need to be able to spend them in my own Dominion."

Klodian reached into a pouch on his belt and produced the coins. He handed them to Mina, and she walked over and gave them to the merchant. The dragon sniffed the air again, and it growled at her, a low rumbling sound deep within its chest.

"Oh, come now Draak. She's harmless."

The dragon hissed and scrambled onto its legs; wings tucked against its body. It ran behind one of the racks and remained there.

"Strange," the merchant said. "I've never seen him do that before."

"It probably doesn't like her stench," Klodian said, shooting a look at Mina. "Thank you for the cinnamon."

"Come back any time!"

They left the tent, joining the other guard on the street.

"Is that the only thing you sense around here?" Klodian asked.

"Yes, my Lord."

Klodian shot her a glare, and she flinched.

"Yes, Ardit."

"Let's walk around to be certain."

Klodian led Mina down more streets than she could count, and eventually, she quit trying to keep track of them. Karapen was a strange and mystifying city. There were more wondrous things and people in this one place than she ever imagined possible, but she didn't sense anything other than the dragon, and that was only when she was close enough to feel the pull from the scale in her leg.

After several hours, Klodian grew irritated and called an end to his test. They stopped at a food stall and he bought them all a slice of dried meat, then they returned to the carriage outside the city. Mina chewed on the treat, which was slightly tough. It was seasoned and tasted good, but it took a decent amount of effort to tear through it with her teeth.

Lord Klodian took the jar of cinnamon from the guard and tossed it to the ground. The glass shattered and the cinnamon scattered across the sand. Mina risked a glance at him, wondering why he did that.

"That man is a fool if he thinks that dragon won't eat him the moment it has the opportunity. Can you believe he said they were intelligent?"

The two guards chuckled. Mina smiled, silently agreeing that the man's words were hard to believe.

"Back to the castle," Klodian said. "This was a wasted trip."

They climbed into the carriage and began the trek back to Klodian Keep. The further away from Karapen they traveled, the more Mina grew uneasy. She looked out the carriage window, but there was nothing to see.

But she *felt* it.

There was a dragon nearby, and it wasn't the same one from the city. Each one had a unique feel to it, and she'd never felt the same one twice. In all the years she'd been leading Klodian on his hunts, he had never failed to slay a dragon. She knew that it was because of his rune magic. Since he was able to draw on the strength of his soldiers, among other traits, he was stronger and faster than his prey.

And yet, despite the many dragons that had fallen to his blade, they still hadn't encountered the one that had cursed her. At least, that's what she hoped. If the dragon had been killed already, that meant its curse had outlasted its existence. And Mina couldn't bear the thought of being a slave her entire life.

"My Lord," she said, keeping her gaze out the window. "There's a dragon nearby."

Klodian tilted his head to look out the window.

"Which direction?"

"I'm not sure. It feels like it's right on top of us. Maybe if we stop, I can get a better sense of where it's at."

Klodian was silent for a moment. "No. We're still too far from the castle for the magic to be effective. I didn't bring my plate armor, either. This one can count itself lucky."

Mina frowned in disappointment. If only Lord Klodian wasn't one of the few who hunted dragons. Aside from the danger, there was only a handful of Dominion Lords. And since rune magic was only for the ruling class, the risk far outweighed the benefit for most people. That's what Mina believed, anyway.

The pull of the scale started to fade, and Mina searched the sky again. This time, she saw something. A massive dark shape shot through the sky heading west. Mina watched until it was no longer visible, her brows furrowed.

She'd never seen a black dragon before.

14

"I want to see what you've got," Captain Eduard said, his arms folded across his chest. He looked at the line of Runesmen.

"It's one thing to swing a sword around in practice, and another to battle a real enemy. Today you will pair up and you will fight. I want you to hold nothing back, but don't kill your partner. A few cuts and scrapes can be dealt with, and they'll heal. If you mortally wound your partner, you will be punished and sent to the gallows. I don't want that, and neither should any of you."

Caden had some skill with a blade, but he wasn't the best by any means. He was eager to learn from someone with more expertise. Not only would it make him a better warrior, but it would also help if he transferred to a Dominion where he would see plenty of battles.

"Thais, you're with Caden."

Eduard flicked his eyes at Caden momentarily before continuing down the line. Caden got the hint, but he wasn't going to let Thais beat him. He drew his sword and took a few steps back, swinging the blade around a few times to loosen his muscles.

Thais drew her sword, a scowl plastered across her face. She looked just like she had the other day when he'd met her. He'd already apologized. What more did she want?

"I hope you don't mind having a few scars across your face," she said smugly.

Caden groaned inwardly. He wasn't vain by any means, but that didn't mean he wanted to look like a veteran of war at such a young age. Without any warning, Thais rushed him, bringing her sword down in an overhead chopping motion. Caden sidestepped and turned to strike her, but she'd already corrected herself and blocked his blade. Metal clanged loudly as their swords clashed, and the two stepped away from each other.

"I said I was sorry," Caden said. "I didn't mean to hurt your feelings."

Thais laughed. "Oh, you thought you hurt my feelings? Please. I don't have any!"

She rushed him again, but this time Caden was prepared. He brought his sword up horizontally, blocking her attack. He allowed her momentum to force his blade downward, but he twisted his wrist at the last moment, causing her to lean far forward. The tip of her sword struck the ground, and Caden lunged forward, jabbing his blade at her ribcage. She was protected by her armor, but he scored a hit.

Thais growled and jerked her sword up, swiping at him. There was a rage in her eyes, and Caden feared that her anger might override her better judgment. She crashed into him, and the next thing he knew, he was lying flat on his back. He stared up at her in confusion, wondering how he had gotten on the ground.

"Very good, Thais," Captain Eduard

congratulated. He stood over Caden and offered his hand. Caden took it and was pulled to his feet.

"Do you know why Thais knocked you down?"

"Because she ran into me?"

"Yes, and no," Eduard said. "That is *how* she knocked you down, but not why. She is brash. She saw an opening and took it, but there is a difference between calculated risk and being reckless. You could have maneuvered out of her path, but you stayed put. Why?"

"I didn't think she could hit that hard," Caden replied.

"You underestimated your opponent. If this were a real battle, you'd be dead because of that error. We are taught when we are young that mistakes are bad, and we are punished for them. Remember this: mistakes are only bad if you don't learn anything from them. Making mistakes is often the best way to learn."

Eduard leaned close to Caden and lowered his voice.

"Thais is skilled and uses her fury to her advantage, but she does have weaknesses. Find them and take a risk."

"Yes, sir."

Eduard stepped back several paces.

"Go again."

Caden and Thais circled one another again, but this time, Caden felt less prepared. Moments ago,

Eduard has accused him of treachery, and now he was offering helpful advice. The man was as confusing as Thais. Caden quickly cleared his mind and silently counted to three, then rushed at Thais. She smiled at him, and before he could bring his sword up to strike her, she dodged to the side, slapping the flat of her blade against the back of his thigh. Stinging pain shot through his leg. He gritted his teeth and whirled around to face her.

"You're so predictable," she taunted.

Caden ignored her words. He could feel Eduard watching him, judging him. Was he regretting his decision to let Caden be a Runesman? Gods, he hoped not. This was his only gateway to the money and fame he wanted, but Lord Klodian's army was ultimately a stepping stone to his end goal. He couldn't afford to stumble on this stone.

"You talk too much," Caden said, slowly closing the distance between them.

Thais didn't wait for him to get close enough. She charged him, swinging her sword in an upward motion. Caden deflected the strike out wide with his blade, then dropped low and slammed the hilt into the side of her knee. She cried out in surprise and fell to the ground.

"How was that for predictable?" he asked as Thais rolled onto her back.

She shot him a glare and rubbed her knee. Caden knew she was angry. She hadn't anticipated his move, and she didn't like losing. He offered her his hand as Eduard had done for him, but she slapped it away and stood on her own.

"Best two out of three," she snapped.

"Fine by me," Caden replied.

He tilted his head from side to side, stretching his neck. There was nothing to gain from this victory. If anything, it would show Captain Eduard that he had learned something. Thais wouldn't be happy about losing, but there was no helping that. She was staring at him, and he stared back, their eyes locked.

At the same time, they ran toward each other. Their blades clanged together, and they began a dance of footwork and flurried jabs and swings. Caden threw everything he had into his maneuvers, pouring every ounce of strength, speed, and mental focus into the fight.

He wasn't her equal. No, she was more skilled than he was, but he managed to hold his own against her until the very end when he saw the weakness that Eduard had told him existed. If she had the slightest hint of what he was thinking, she could easily block him and win. And if she didn't, then he would be the victor. He kept her busy with his thrusts, but his muscles burned and his stamina was failing. Eduard had told him to take a risk. It was now or never. Caden waited until he saw Thais overextend herself as she jabbed her blade at him, then he smacked her sword up high and quickly stepped forward. He came in low and drove his shoulder into her stomach.

She grunted in surprise and pain, and his

momentum pushed her off balance. She staggered backward and fell, crashing to the ground with a loud thud. He put his foot on her chest, pinning her down, and placed the tip of his sword against her neck.

"Do you yield?" he asked.

Her eyes welled with tears, but he doubted they were from embarrassment. She'd fallen hard and he was certain she was in pain. She gasped her answer, making him the winner of their bout. He removed his sword and turned to look at Captain Eduard. The other Runesmen had gathered to watch their battle, and they started cheering.

"You took a risk," Eduard said. "She left an opening and you went for it. She could have had you."

"I know. I was afraid that my eyes would give me away, but she was too consumed with emotion. It worked to my advantage."

"Congratulations. You learned something new today."

Eduard spun on the others. "The show's over. Get back to it!"

The Runesmen went back to sparring, and Caden looked at Thais. She was on her feet now, and she sheathed her blade. She limped over to him and clapped him on the shoulder.

"I'm impressed," she said. "You beat me fairly, but it won't happen again."

"We'll see," Caden replied.

"Yes, we will." Thais lowered her voice. "I still think you should tell him what you found."

"I'm not going to."

"Suit yourself." Thais shrugged. "It's your funeral if I'm right."

She headed for the barracks, and as she hobbled away, Caden felt guilty for hitting her so hard in the knee, but when he considered the rage he'd seen in her eyes, he knew she would have done the same thing.

If not worse.

15

It had been a week since the attack on Slia.

Lord Klodian was just as fixated on revenge as he had been the day it happened, and Mina felt as if she were on the brink of exhaustion. Every day since then, Klodian had taken her on his hunts. They searched the desert plateaus, scoured the hidden caves, and trekked across the dry landscape for hours.

Granted, Klodian had killed more dragons in the last few days than he had the entire previous summer, but Mina was tired. Her skin was sunburned so much that it had blistered, and when she was sweating, the water collected beneath her flesh and made her feel like some sort of monster.

They returned every night in time for dinner, and this night was no different. Since they spent the entire day hunting, Klodian didn't make her complete her usual chores. The evenings were hers to do as she wished, and she'd been spending them in the field outside the castle, staring up at the stars.

Mina was lying in the dry grass, her stomach full. She wanted to rest, but for some reason, sleep eluded her. She had much on her mind, and it all haunted her as she lay there in the quiet of the night. Distant memories, hopes, and nightmares all barraged her. The chirping of some sort of animal in the distance crept into her ears, bringing with it madness and the desperation to make it disappear.

Above her, the night sky was clear and the stars glimmered brightly. She traced the constellation Avera with her eyes, wondering who had been the first to spot the human shape the stars formed. Avera was the goddess of fortune, and Mina had prayed to her many times when she was younger. That was before she knew the truth, that there were no gods. Or, if there were, the plight of the people mattered little to them. The sound of someone approaching broke her reverie, and she lifted her head to see Caden.

"Another quiet night," he said softly. "And another quiet shift."

He took a seat beside her and leaned back, propping himself up with his arms. He looked into the sky, and she stared at his face. He was a handsome man, but she knew that Thais desired him. It was obvious in the way she acted around him. Mina didn't mind. She wanted her freedom from the cursed scale, and the desire for romance would only detract her attention from what mattered.

She considered him a friend, though. She'd never really had many, at least not since she was a child. Before her accident, she'd had a few friends. Once word spread of the scale in her leg, she became shunned by everyone. Mina found navigating a friendship more difficult than she remembered, but she knew that Caden didn't plan on staying in the Thophate Dominion.

"Do you ever question yourself?" Mina asked.

"All the time," Caden replied. "Why?"

"I don't know. I guess I'm just curious if I'm the only one that does it."

Caden laughed and turned to look at her. "Everyone wonders whether they are on the right path at some point. Nobody is perfect."

"Some people make it seem as if they have everything planned out and their life is perfect. Like you."

"Me? My life is hardly perfect."

"Isn't it, though? Your dream was to become a Runesman, and you are one."

"Yes, but it took a lot of effort to get here. And being a Runesman is only part of what I want. I want to be wealthy. I want people to know my name, but not because of anything I've done wrong, but for the fact that a lowly peasant lifted himself out of poverty and into grandeur. To do that, I'll have to keep from dying."

"I've seen you fight," Mina said. "You're very good."

"To the untrained eye, perhaps." Caden smiled. "I'm not one of the best with a sword in my group, let alone the entire army."

"And yet you were put on guard duty so quickly."

"Only because of the circumstances. Lord Klodian has lost four patrols. They've vanished without a trace, and The Long Sands is a big place. We can't go searching for them without risking the loss of more men."

"What do you think happened to them?"

"No idea," Caden replied. "Maybe they defected, but I doubt it. There have been a lot of sand storms recently, so Captain Eduard believes they got lost. If they don't return within a few days, Lord Klodian is going to assume they are dead. Without water, it's impossible to survive out there."

Mina did find the disappearance of the patrols curious, but since it didn't affect her, she hadn't dwelled on it. It must not have bothered Lord Klodian much either, for his focus had been on hunting down dragons.

"Have you ever seen a dragon?" she asked.

"No. And I don't think I want to."

She didn't blame him. They were ferocious, and any creature that could breathe fire didn't seem like a natural creation.

"When do you think you'll go to another Dominion?"

Caden shrugged. "Captain Eduard thinks I had something to do with Lord Klodian being unconscious after the attack in Slia. Until I can prove I didn't and get in his good graces, it's probably wise not to mention it."

"I didn't know that. Why does he think it was you?"

"I was the first one to find him, so he thinks it's suspicious. If Thais and I wouldn't have split up, I doubt it would be an issue. Regardless, I'm going to work as hard as I can to show my devotion. Lord Klodian seems like a good man, but there's no way I'll find what I'm looking for out here in the desert."

"There is a way," Mina said. "But it requires slaying dragons."

"No thank you. I prefer the odds against other people, not oversized living cauldrons. Maybe if you come up with something less dangerous, I'll consider it."

It was Mina's turn to laugh. She did that often in Caden's presence, which was another thing she wasn't accustomed to.

"You may not want to see a dragon, but what about a dragon's horn?"

"Why would I want to see a dragon's horn?"

"I have a collection. Lord Klodian cuts one off of each dragon he kills and gives it to me. He knows I hate them, and I think in some small way, it's a sign of kindness from him." She didn't mention that it was the *only* kindness he showed her.

"Where do you keep them?"

"Under my bed," Mina answered.

"You know Runesmen aren't allowed in the castle except for meals, right?"

"I'm sorry, it was stupid of me to ask."

"Don't apologize," Caden said. "It's not stupid. I'd love to see them, but I don't want to break the rules. Could you bring them out here?"

"No, the chest I keep them in is too heavy. Just forget it. I don't want to get you into trouble."

The silence stretched between them until Caden finally spoke.

"I'll go if you really want me to."

It wasn't what he said, but the *way* he said it that caused Mina's heart to race. She only wanted to show him her collection, but the tone in his voice set a fire under her skin that she couldn't explain. She knew it was a bad idea, but maybe if she showed him quickly, he wouldn't be caught. The servants would still be working, so there wouldn't be anyone in the room yet. Mina stood and motioned for him.

"Let's go."

16

Caden followed Mina into the castle, ducking into doorways and side passages as they passed by servants who were still working. He wasn't wearing his armor, and it was dark, but he didn't want to take any chances. If someone recognized him and informed Captain Eduard, or worse—Lord Klodian—he'd surely be lashed again. While the wounds would heal, the pain wasn't something he relished. After traversing numerous maze-like halls, he was growing worried.

"How much further?" he whispered.

"Not much. It's just around the corner now. Stay here and let me make sure it's clear."

Mina disappeared from sight and he glanced back the way they'd come. The longer he spent inside the castle, the more he feared he would be caught. Footsteps echoed off the walls, but he didn't know which direction they were coming from. Caden moved into a darkened doorway and stood still.

A servant came around the corner, where Mina had gone. The woman carried a candle on a small plate and passed by without seeing him, continuing down the hall, her steps fading. A moment later, Mina returned.

"Sorry," she said softly. "Kera was in there, so I told her that she was needed in the kitchens.

Hopefully, they'll put her to work, but she might be back soon. We probably don't have much time. Come on."

Mina led him around the corner and into a large chamber filled with beds. At the end of each one was a large chest, which he presumed was for personal effects. The setup was very similar to the barracks, including the windows. Moonlight filtered into the room, providing plenty of light.

"I don't know why, but I just assumed the servants all had their own rooms," Caden said.

"I wish," Mina replied. "It's hard to sleep when there are so many people snoring at the same time."

Mina walked over to a cot that was against the far wall and knelt beside it. She leaned down and reached under the bed, sliding a plain wooden box out. It was smaller than the chest, but it was still a decent size. She stood and hefted the box onto the bed, opening the lid. Caden moved to stand beside her and glanced inside. Horns of all sizes rested inside, all stacked in neat rows, and they were all the same color.

"That's a lot of dead dragons," Caden said.

"It is, but it's not enough."

"Will it ever be?"

Mina went quiet for a moment. She turned her head to him. "It will be enough when this curse is gone."

Caden was tempted to ask her what she would

do if the curse was never lifted, but he didn't want to upset her. She seemed proud of the horns. In a way, he understood why. She hated dragons with a passion, but she was also responsible for their deaths. Lord Klodian might be the one who killed them, but she played a large part by tracking them down.

"Aren't dragons different colors?"

"Yes," Mina answered.

"Then why are the horns all the same color?"

Mina shrugged. "I'm not sure why, but color of the horn fades once it's removed. There is a way to tell what color the dragon was, though." She grabbed one of the horns and angled the pointed end down, revealing the end that had been cut. It was smooth, but Caden noticed something else. The color on the inside was gold.

"The inside of their horns mirrors the color of their scales. This one was a gold dragon."

"How many colors are there?"

"Five that I know of. Gold, silver, bronze, brass, and copper." Mina paused, and Caden had the feeling she wanted to say more.

"Do you have horns from all the colors?"

"No. I have a horn from each one except copper. Copper dragons seem to be rarer than the others."

"You seem to know a lot about them."

"There isn't much to know, really. They're wild and untamed like any other animal, just bigger and meaner."

"Well, I'm glad I've never seen one," Caden said. "I imagine it's frightening."

"Very," Mina replied. "I've only seen a few of them. They're usually hiding in caves, and Lord Klodian kills them before I ever see them. The last one I saw made my entire body shake, and it wasn't even looking at me."

Caden knew the term for it: dragon fear. It was an overwhelming sense of irrational dread. At least, that's how he'd heard it explained. There weren't many who encountered a dragon and lived to tell of it.

"What will you do when the curse is lifted?" Caden changed the subject.

"Lord Klodian will have no use for me, so he'll either sell me or grant me my freedom. I've more than returned the investment he paid my parents. If he sells me, I'll run away, probably go to a new Dominion. Who knows, maybe I'll end up at the same one you transfer to." She smiled.

Caden doubted that Lord Klodian would grant Mina her freedom. He probably *would* sell her—to the highest bidder and then forget about her. He hoped that whatever happened, she wouldn't be hurt. There were a lot of unscrupulous people in the world, and many of them lacked the decency that Lord Klodian had. Caden didn't know Mina very well, but she deserved more from life than being a slave.

Mina met his gaze and they stared at each other in silence. He was drawn to her, like a moth to the flame. He was also drawn to Thais, and he could feel his heart warring within him. Both women were beautiful, and his feelings toward each were different, but his emotions were a confusing muddle.

Without much thought, he leaned toward Mina and kissed her. Her lips were soft, and she smelled of dust and something pleasant, but he couldn't place the scent. She didn't return the kiss, and he feared he had crossed a line with her. He broke away and smiled despite the fact that his heart raced with nervousness.

"Good night," he said, then turned and left.

He hurried down the hall and quickly realized he had no idea how to get out of the castle. Mina herself had seemed unsure of which halls to take, and it wasn't long before he was lost. It didn't help that he couldn't focus on finding the right path. His thoughts were on Mina. Had he offended her with his kiss, or had he merely surprised her? He prayed it was the latter.

Caden turned a corner and bumped into the servant he'd seen earlier. Mina had said her name was Kera. She curtsied and cast her eyes to the floor.

"Excuse me, my Lord. I wasn't watching where I was going."

It felt odd to have someone called him that. He offered his best smile and tried to keep from stammering.

"It's not a problem. I'm trying to get some fresh air in the courtyard, but I seem to have gotten turned around. Can you direct me?"

"Of course, my Lord. I'll show you the way."

Kera navigated the maze easily and once they passed the dining hall, he recognized his surroundings.

"Ah, I know my way from here. Thank you."

"Of course, my Lord. It was my honor."

He waited until she was gone, then he hurriedly escaped the castle and breathed a sigh of relief once he was outside. The air was cool and he relaxed his pace. As the excitement of the kiss faded, he felt guilty. It wasn't just that he'd kissed Mina without her permission, but he felt as if he'd somehow betrayed Thais. It was foolish of him to feel that way since he and Thais hadn't even discussed their feelings, but the guilt assailed him nonetheless.

The barracks was dark when he entered, but he could tell that most of his fellows were still awake. Caden reached his cot and laid down without taking his shoes off. He was floating somewhere between the clouds of tranquility and remorse. He should tell Thais what he'd done. She would probably be mad, but his conscience would be clear. Telling the truth was never easy, but it was the right thing to do.

Before he could sit up, a commotion near the entrance drew his attention. Captain Eduard and two others marched inside, waving torches around.

"Where's Caden?" Eduard demanded.

"I'm here, sir."

Caden rolled off the cot and stood at attention. Eduard and the other two came straight toward him.

"You're under arrest," Eduard said. "Take him to the dungeon."

"Arrest? For what?" Caden looked from Eduard to the guards as if the answer would be evident on their faces.

"I know what you did. There's no sense in feigning ignorance. That'll just make it worse. Take him."

The guards forcibly turned him around and bound his hands with rope, then hooked their arms with his and marched him through the barracks toward the door. Caden didn't understand what Eduard was talking about. He hadn't done anything wrong. Had he?

As they passed Thais's cot, she was standing beside it. Caden looked at her pleadingly, and she mouthed the words, "I'm sorry."

17

Caden's kiss haunted her.

Mina had never been kissed before, and the experience left her reeling and flustered. Her emotions were a confusing mess. She'd assumed that he had feelings for Thais, but clearly, she'd been mistaken. Caden was handsome and well-muscled, but she hadn't thought about him as anything more than a friend.

No, that wasn't entirely true. Mina was lying to herself, and she knew it. Perhaps it was the fear of the unknown that held her back, but she didn't want Caden to be more than a friend. There were too many things to consider.

He was a Runesman, first and foremost. His life would always be in jeopardy. She was a slave to Lord Klodian. Outside of his whims, she didn't have much control over her life. Not yet, anyway. And there was no way for her to know when she might be free ... if she ever would be. Dreams were one thing, but reality was another.

Caden also wanted to leave the Thophate Dominion. If he left, Mina wouldn't be able to follow him unless she gained her freedom. Not without incurring Klodian's wrath, and she knew he would stop at nothing to find her if she ran away. His hunts and his wealth were too important to him.

Mina stared at the collection of horns in the

chest for a moment before closing the lid. Some of the servants would give her odd looks when she was brought them out to look at them, but they didn't understand. It wasn't for some morbid fascination that she kept them. They were trophies, the spoils of her personal war against dragons.

"No one will ever understand," she whispered.

Mina placed the chest on the floor and slid it under the bed. She hoped Caden had found his way out of the castle. It had been tempting to race after him, but she knew that Kera could return at any time. If Caden was caught breaking the rules, Mina would feel terrible. She'd convinced him to come into the castle, so any punishment he received would be her fault.

She sat on the bed and pulled her boots off. Relief flooded through her feet. Lord Klodian had been relentless the last few days, scouring the desert for dragons. Tomorrow would be no different. She sighed and laid down, staring up at the dark ceiling.

The next thing she knew, a faint light was filtering through the windows. She'd fallen asleep and she assumed she hadn't moved all night, as she was in the same position she remembered being in when she'd been thinking about Caden. With the sun rising, Lord Klodian would be readying to leave. Mina rubbed her eyes and sat up, sliding her legs off the edge of the bed. She pulled her boots on and decided to go to the barracks to see Caden before she left.

Since it was still early, the castle was silent.

Most of the servants were still asleep, and Mina didn't pass anyone in the halls. She left the castle and crossed the courtyard, quietly entering the barracks. The Runesmen would be up soon to begin their next day of training, and Mina didn't want to be in the middle of the chaos.

She searched the rows of cots, but she didn't see Caden anywhere. Had he started his run around the castle early? She paused, glancing around the barracks.

"What are you doing?" Thais whispered.

Mina whirled around, her heart racing. Thais was sitting on her cot, staring at Mina.

"I was looking for Caden."

"I figured as much. He's not here."

"Is he running his laps?"

Thais shook her head. "He's in the dungeon," she replied. "Captain Eduard arrested him last night."

Mina's eyes widened. "What? Why?"

Thais shrugged. "If anyone knows, they aren't saying. Eduard hauled him off and we haven't seen or heard from either of them since."

Mina needed to find out what happened, but it would have to wait. Lord Klodian was probably waiting on her by now. "If you hear anything, please let me know. I'll do the same for you."

"Sounds fair to me."

Mina rushed out of the barracks, turning toward the stable. Just as she suspected, Lord Klodian was waiting for her when she arrived. Vhan was there as well, but none of the usual entourage was present.

"If you oversleep again, I'll drag you behind my horse," Klodian threatened.

"I'm sorry, my Lord. It won't happen again."

"See that it doesn't. You'll be riding with Vhan today. You've been walking too slow lately, and I need to get back earlier tonight. I have matters to deal with."

Mina nodded, relieved to know that they wouldn't be spending the entire day in the heat again. She walked over to Vhan's horse, and the squire offered his hand to her, pulling her into the saddle behind him. It was an uncomfortable spot to sit, but she was happy that she didn't have to go on foot.

They rode northwest, heading in the same direction they had the day before. Mina held onto Vhan to keep from falling off the horse, but he didn't seem to mind. Eventually, Lord Klodian began talking with Vhan. Mina was only half-listening, but it sounded like Klodian's advisors weren't happy with him.

"I'm the lord of this Dominion," Klodian said. "I won't be scolded like a child. If they want to keep complaining, I'll string them all up on the gallows."

"I think they're worried, my Lord." Vhan

replied.

"About what?"

"You, among other things. You haven't hunted dragons this much in all the time I've been alive. And there are the rumors …"

"Bah! Rumors are all they are. War isn't brewing in the Dominions. The High Prince would sweep down from the north with his armies and remind us all quite painfully of how he united the lands in the first place. And as for the dragon hunts, it's nobody's business but my own if I seek revenge on the blasted creatures. They destroyed Slia, and I won't let it be said that I didn't bring hell upon the dragons in response."

"I'm on your side, sir. I want to see justice as much as you."

Mina rubbed her left leg. The scale was giving her something, but it was faint.

"I'm sure you do," Klodian said. "And I appreciate your loyalty. That's why you are with me today and my advisors are not. I'm tired of hearing their constant whining."

"My ears thank you," Vhan replied, laughing.

Lord Klodian looked over at Mina. "Anything?"

"Yes, but it's not very strong yet. Maybe a little further."

Ahead, a mesa towered over the landscape. Mina suspected there was a cave there, since the closer they got, the stronger the sensation became.

Once they were a few hundred feet away, Mina was certain this was it.

"It's here," she said.

The mesa was split in two by a narrow pass. It looked to Mina as though someone had cracked the mesa like an egg. The walls of the pass weren't jagged, though, but instead had a checkered pattern to them.

"The dragon is in there." Mina pointed at the narrow opening between the two massive pieces of the mesa.

They reined the horses to a stop and Lord Klodian dismounted. He grabbed his sword from the saddle and strapped it onto his waist, then looked at Vhan.

"You ready?"

"My Lord?"

"You're coming with me on this one. I want you to witness what it takes to kill one. Even with my runes, they are a challenging foe."

"I've waited a long time for this," Vhan said. He slid out of the saddle and adjusted his chainmail shirt, then looked up at Mina.

"Do you want to stay on the horse?"

"Not really."

Vhan offered her his hand, and she accepted his help with climbing down. Once she was on the ground, Lord Klodian and Vhan walked together into the pass. Mina held the reins of Vhan's horse, running her hands along its soft neck. It nickered softly and nudged her with its nose when she stopped.

"You don't have to be rude," Mina said playfully.

The scale in her leg alerted her to the presence of another dragon. And another. She turned toward the pass and scanned the sky, but there were no dragons flying overhead. There were definitely three. She could feel each one individually. Both horses seemed to grow agitated. They snorted and stamped the ground.

Something was wrong.

Mina didn't know where the other two dragons had come from, but if there were three in the pass, Lord Klodian would be outmatched. She needed to warn him before it was too late, but before she could do anything, Vhan's horse screeched and reared on its hind legs, pulling the reins from her grasp. Mina watched helplessly as both horses turned and bolted off, heading toward the castle.

The scale in her leg thrummed, and she sprinted toward the mesa.

18

Thais had betrayed him.

Her apology was an admission of guilt. The image of her mouthing her contrition had replayed in his mind over and over, keeping him awake most of the night. Not only that, but it had been cold and he didn't have a blanket.

Caden sat on the frigid stone floor of his cell, his back pressed against the wall. His wrists were shackled and chained to the stones behind him. It didn't make any sense. Why would she have ratted him out about what he'd found? And why would Captain Eduard care so much? It was difficult to fathom that Eduard believed Thais's wild conspiracy theory.

Yet here he was in the dungeon.

Approaching footsteps caught his attention. Someone stopped in front of his cell, and Caden squinted, trying to see in the dimness. Keys rattled, and the cell door swung open. A figure stepped inside and paused.

"Hungry?"

It was Captain Eduard. He stepped closer and knelt, offering Caden a tray with a bowl of steaming soup and half a loaf of bread. Caden's stomach rumbled at the sight and he took the tray and began eating. Eduard rose back to his feet and stood there quietly.

"I know what you did," he finally said.

"What's that?"

Eduard half snorted and half laughed. "Are we not adults? Cease the games, Caden. You did something to Lord Klodian in Slia. Just admit it."

Caden licked the warm soup from his lips. "I didn't do anything to Lord Klodian. I told you, I found him unconscious. What would I have to gain by harming him, anyway? It's not like I'm his heir, so I couldn't take his position."

"That is true, but I'm sure you have other motivations. Your loyalty lies elsewhere anyway, does it not?"

"My loyalty lies with you and Lord Klodian," Caden replied. "I've done nothing for you to question that."

Eduard folded his arms and stared at Caden, who in turn continued to eat. He finished off the bread, dipping the last piece in the soup for added flavor.

"I was expecting moldy bread and cold food, to be honest."

"We're not tyrants," Eduard scoffed.

"And I'm thankful for that."

"Which Dominion are you from?"

"This one," Caden said. "I was born here in the Thophate."

"I don't believe you."

"Believe what you will, sir. I have no reason to lie."

"Sure you do. You're a spy from another Dominion, maybe even an assassin. Who sent you here?"

Caden slurped the last of the soup and put the bowl on the tray, then set the tray aside. He wiped his mouth with the back of his hand, the chains clanking with his movements.

"No one sent me here. I'm here of my own choice. I want to be a Runesman. I *am* a Runesman. You saw my value and selected me. Why do you question me now? Because I found Lord Klodian unconscious? Thais and Mina were there with me before we started searching for him. Did you speak to them?"

"I did," Eduard answered. "They seemed forthcoming, but Thais has an attachment to you and Mina is a slave. Her word means nothing."

"What of Thais's word? Does it mean nothing as well? You said yourself that we're a brotherhood. Even if she feels something for me, she wouldn't break her oath as a Runesman."

"Say what you will, but until you admit what you're doing here or prove your innocence, you're going to rot down here."

"How can I prove my innocence? I've told you everything and you have chosen not to believe me."

"I have evidence," Eduard said.

Caden assumed he was talking about the piece of metal he'd found in Slia. If he admitted to finding it, would Eduard release him?

"If you are referring to what I found in Slia, that's not evidence of anything. I found it in the wreckage, and I'm certain it has nothing to do with Thais's theory."

Eduard gave him a hard stare, then unfolded his arms and collected the tray. He walked to the cell door and paused, looking over his shoulder at Caden.

"You'll break eventually," he said. "And when you do, I'll be here to deal out your punishment."

Eduard closed the door behind him and locked it. His steps gradually faded and Caden was left more confused than he'd been before their conversation. Had a spy from another Dominion really infiltrated Lord Klodian's army? And if so, what was their mission? Perhaps if Caden could figure out who it was, he could offer their name to Eduard and secure his release.

Unfortunately, being locked in the dungeon hindered him from gathering information, but on the bright side, he had plenty of time to think. He began to analyze everything he knew about his fellow Runesmen. He replayed conversations, trying to find something, anything, that seemed suspicious, and he came up with … much of nothing.

As far as he could tell, everyone that had joined Lord Klodian's army at the same time as him seemed legitimate. Captain Eduard had to be wrong.

That, or he'd said all those things merely to mess with his mind. Caden heaved a sigh and rested his head against the wall. He didn't want to spend the rest of his days in the dungeon, but without help from someone, he feared that would be his fate.

19

Mina stepped into the entrance of the pass, trying to be as quiet as possible. She didn't hear the sound of fighting, and the passage that cleaved through the mesa twisted and turned, making it impossible to see what lay ahead. She hoped the silence didn't bode something bad.

The walls of the mesa stretched upward, towering high above her. Small crevices broke off to the left and right, but they were too small to enter. In the sand, two sets of footprints were clearly visible. Lord Klodian's tracks were obviously the larger of the two, and she followed the same path.

Mina could feel three distinct dragons through the scale, though one felt much stronger than the others. They were all close, too close for her comfort, but if she didn't warn Klodian before he stumbled upon them, she'd be returning to the castle alone. Of course, that would mean she was free from slavery, but she wanted to be free of the cursed scale more.

A roar filled the air, echoing off the walls. The sound was so powerful that Mina paused and almost fled. A feeling of dread washed over her, but something deep down made her continue walking. There was a metallic clang, followed by a human scream full of pain. Mina steeled herself against her fear and peered around the curved wall. The narrow passage opened up into a large space, and her eyes widened.

There were three enormous copper dragons. They were all equal in size, but the one in the center was the one that Mina could feel the strongest through the scale. A row of spines trailed from its head down its back, each one growing smaller as they reached the tail. Two long, curved horns swooped back from either side of its head, and on the tips of its wings were smaller horns.

Claws as long as daggers gouged the dirt as it stepped. Its mouth was open, saliva dripping from its teeth. And then Mina noticed Lord Klodian on the ground in front of the dragon. His sword was lying a few feet away, and he was crawling backward like a crab. She assumed he was injured by the way he was moving, and she looked for Vhan.

The squire was near one of the other dragons, but unlike Klodian, he wasn't moving. A dark puddle surrounded his body and Mina feared that the boy was dead. She didn't know what to do. Going back to the castle to get help wasn't an option. Even if the horses hadn't run off, it was too far.

Kill him.

Mina whirled around to see who was behind her, but the passage was empty. She'd heard a voice. Where had it come from?

Yes, kill him.

A second voice.

Mina looked up, but there was nothing but the blue sky overhead. Was she losing her mind? Had the curse finally taken its toll on her? What was happening?

Don't worry, brethren. The dragon slayer will die, but I want to see him squirm.

Mina froze. A hundred thoughts became a tangled mess within her mind. She slowly peered around the corner again. The dragon in the center stalked toward Klodian. Was she hearing the dragons? No, that wasn't possible. Dragons couldn't speak. They were mindless animals. They—

There's another one nearby. Hurry, brother! Before more of them show up.

The dragon that was stalking Klodian issued a throaty growl and lunged forward. Klodian dropped down flat, and the dragon's maw full of razor-sharp teeth narrowly missed him. Mina's heart leaped in her chest. This was it. Klodian was going to die. He lifted an arm as if he could block the powerful creature. When Mina stepped into their line of sight, she had no idea why she did it.

"Stop!"

All three dragons whipped their heads in her direction, and she realized she'd made a terrible mistake. Now they would all be dragon food.

It's a female. It was the dragon on the left.

A brave one. This from the one on the right.

Mina had no idea how she knew which one was speaking, she just *knew*. Perhaps it was the scale. Or perhaps she was hallucinating this entire situation. Yes, maybe the heat had gotten to her and she was actually passed out on Vhan's horse, feverishly dreaming all of this.

She will die like the dragon slayer. The leader of the group. The one she felt the strongest connection to. His presence seemed larger than life, and she thought she could feel hints of emotions and thoughts from him. He was mostly angry, but there was a hint of hunger underneath, and it was all wrapped in fear. Fear? The dragon was afraid? Of what? And why?

Time seemed to stand still. Mina stood in place, dragon fear overtaking her. She'd never been this close to one. Perhaps that's why she could hear their thoughts. She tried to move, but she was frozen with terror. The leader spread his talons and slammed his front right claw over Klodian, pinning him in place.

Mina wanted to scream, but she couldn't move her mouth. Her muscles refused to obey her will. The dragon lowered his head down, mere inches from Klodian's face. The air from the dragon's nostrils ruffled Klodian's hair, and the Dominion Lord struggled against the dragon's claw.

Justice has come for this human, killer of dragons.

May he never find rest, even in death, the other two chimed in unison.

The leader opened his jaws. Mina still couldn't move, so she did the only thing she could think of. She screamed as loud as she could within her mind, directing it at the sensations she felt from the scale in her leg.

Don't kill him!

The dragon leader stiffened, his fiery gaze landing on her. The other two dragons slowly stepped backward, and she could *smell* their fear. It was the scent of lavender. Mina didn't have time to consider how she could smell their fear. Her terror dissipated and she lifted her right hand into the air.

Don't kill him! She shouted again. The two dragons snorted and unfurled their wings. They clawed their way up the sides of the mesa and launched themselves into the air. The leader regarded her warily, and the lavender scent poured from him. Mina took a step forward and the dragon tensed.

Flee! Mina demanded.

The dragon stared at her, its eyes looking her up and down. Its gaze stopped on her leg, and Mina's cheeks flushed. It seemed even dragons judged her deformity. The dragon suddenly drew back and climbed the mesa wall, following after the other two. It leaped into the air and stretched out its wings, flapping them and gaining altitude. Despite being up as high as it was, the air from its wings stirred the sand in the clearing. Mina buried her face in the crook of her arm and waited until the dust settled, then rushed over to Klodian. She lifted the visor on his helm and met his eyes.

"You saved my life," he breathed.

She'd done it for selfish reasons, but he didn't need to know that. He was her key to freedom from the curse, which was made worse now that she knew she could hear dragons.

"We need to get you back to the castle," she said. "Can you walk? The horses are gone."

"I can manage. I'll use the runes if I need to."

Mina grabbed onto his hand and pulled with all her might. He got on his feet and Mina started to walk toward Vhan.

"Leave him," Klodian said. "He's dead."

"Are you sure, my Lord?"

"Not even I could have survived what happened to him."

Mina walked over to Vhan anyway, kneeling beside him and trying not to look at the gruesomeness. His eyes were open and staring off. Klodian was right. He *was* dead. She pressed her fingertips to his eyelids and gently closed them.

"Find rest in the spirit world," she said softly.

She rose and returned to Klodian's side, and they traversed the passage out of the mesa. Mina kept glancing skyward, but there was no sign of the dragons. She could still feel the powerful leader through the scale in her leg and she looked back at the mesa. He was probably hiding there, watching them.

"What is it?" Klodian asked.

"Nothing," Mina replied. "I'm just nervous."

"I owe you a debt, Mina. Consider what you want. No matter what it is, it shall be yours."

There were many things that Mina wanted, but at that moment, there was only one that mattered. As they trudged across the desert back to the castle, she realized that, for the first time, Klodian had called her by her name.

20

The jingling of keys roused Caden from his stupor.

He blinked several times, wondering if the sound was real or part of the daydream he'd been entertaining. When the lock clicked and the cell door swung open, he had his answer. Captain Eduard stepped inside, and he didn't look happy.

The small rectangular window high above him allowed just enough light into the cell for him to see that Eduard had a bundle of clothes tucked under his arm. The man's jaw was clenched, and he walked over to the cot and set the clothes down, then unlocked the shackles from Caden's wrists.

"What's going on?" Caden asked.

"You're being transferred to another Dominion, per Lord Klodian's orders."

Caden absently rubbed his sore wrists. He was being transferred? A multitude of questions tumbled around within his mind. Transferring to another Dominion had been his goal when he first became a Runesman over a week ago, but now he was having second thoughts. Being around Thais and Mina had made him question that goal, and he was now more conflicted than ever.

"I … don't understand," he said.

"There's no need to. It's Lord Klodian's

bidding, and so it will be done. Get dressed. When you're done, you'll collect your things from the barracks and be on your way."

Eduard stepped out of the cell and hovered in the hallway. Caden didn't want to question his luck, and he quickly changed into the clean clothes Eduard had provided. They weren't his own, but they fit well enough. He tossed the dirty rags he'd been wearing onto the cot, stretched his muscles, then joined Eduard in the hall.

"Follow me."

Caden did as he was asked and trailed Eduard out of the dungeon and into the castle. They didn't talk at all, and Caden was beginning to understand that whatever had transpired between Eduard and Lord Klodian wasn't what Eduard wanted. They exited the castle and Caden breathed in a deep breath of fresh air. He hadn't been in the dungeon long, but the stench had been overwhelming. Unbathed bodies and the desert heat were a bad combination.

The two marched across the courtyard and into the barracks. The other Runesmen were out training, and the building was empty. Caden went to his cot and gathered his meager belongings, which were nothing more than two sets of clothing, a small bag of silver coins, and the piece of metal he'd found in Slia. He stuffed them all into a leather bag and turned to Eduard.

"Can I say goodbye to a few people?"

"No."

Judging by his tone, Caden knew there was no room for debate. He nodded, not bothering to argue.

"What Dominion am I being transferred to?"

"The Dracan Dominion. It's northeast of here. You'll be given a horse, so you should get there within a few days. If you ride hard, you can make it in two."

The Dracan Dominion. Caden knew it. Everyone did. It was home to Lord Kristofel D'Lance, right hand to the High Prince himself. He boasted the largest army and had more land than any other Dominion Lord. It all confused Caden even more. The move should be for someone esteemed, not a neophyte Runesman like himself. Was his transfer a punishment, or a reward?

"One of the patrols will escort you to the border, then you are on your own from there."

"May I speak bluntly, sir?"

"You may."

"I know you still think I did something to Lord Klodian, and outside of one of the gods themselves coming to you to say otherwise, I know you won't change your mind about that. I stand by my words. I didn't do anything to him, I swear it. I don't know why I'm being transferred, but if we never meet again, I want you to know I don't hold any grudge against you. If I were in your shoes, I would believe whatever my feelings were too, but sometimes the things that seem right couldn't be further from the truth."

Captain Eduard cleared his throat.

"You're a good soldier, there's no mistaking that. Whether my suspicions are true or not doesn't matter now. You're no longer under my command. Is that everything, then?"

"Yes, sir."

"Good. Come on."

They went to the stable and Caden was surprised to find that a horse had already been readied for him. The mount was saddled and a satchel of provisions had been strapped to it. He was being transferred, given a horse and provisions, and this was somehow a punishment? Caden smiled to himself. Perhaps a fresh start was in his best interest. A clean slate in a new Dominion could be just what he needed.

Caden strapped his bag to the saddle and mounted the horse. Eduard stared up at him, and he had the feeling that the captain wanted to say something. The man remained silent, however.

"Let the winds blow in your favor to keep the dust from your eyes," Caden said.

"May the sun be at your back so that you always see your enemies," Eduard replied.

Caden took the reins in his hands and flicked them, guiding the horse toward the gates. Once he was outside the castle walls, he spotted the patrol Eduard had mentioned. The small group was waiting on him, and as he joined their ranks, they turned northeast and began the trek toward the border.

He didn't know any of the other Runesmen. They were his seniors, and they all had scars from countless battles. They must have transferred from other Dominions because it was well known that Lord Klodian rarely waged war against his fellow lords. As he considered the proverbial road ahead, he was excited. It was a chance to prove himself a capable soldier, and to find the fame and riches he'd wanted for as long as he could remember.

While the opportunity was good, he hated how it had all happened. Thais had betrayed his trust, forcing him to lose her and Mina all in one fell swoop. He hoped that Thais felt guilty. A sudden wave of anger washed over him, and he cursed her. She'd ruined things for him, and not just with Captain Eduard. He'd lost Mina as well. Caden knew the sting of her treachery would fade, but his memory of her actions would not.

As the seed of hatred began to sprout within him, he silently prayed that he would meet Thais on the battlefield one day. He couldn't right her wrong, but he could avenge himself.

And he *would* avenge himself.

21

Mina walked with hesitant steps into Lord Klodian's personal chamber. He'd summoned her, and she wasn't sure if that was a good thing. She'd saved his life, true, but since he was a Dominion Lord, he owed her nothing. It was a miracle that he had granted her anything at all, but she felt confident that she'd used her favor toward a good purpose.

Lord Klodian was at his desk, flipping through parchments and muttering to himself. Mina stood to the side and waited, but he was completely enveloped in his work. She didn't want to interrupt him, but he had asked her to come to see him. Her palms were sweating with her nervousness, and she cleared her throat.

The sound caused Klodian to look up and he frowned at her. She swallowed hard, thinking he was upset with her.

"If you are busy, I can come back later, my Lord."

"What? Oh. No. No, now is fine."

He rose from his chair and came to stand in front of her. Even without his armor, he was an imposing figure. He was taller than Caden. He was more muscular, too, and his physique was more noticeable when he wore plain clothes. Tinges of gray interspersed with his brown hair, and his blue eyes were as hard as steel.

"I wanted you to know that your request for your friend to be transferred to another Dominion has been completed."

"Thank you, my Lord."

"It's the least I can do to repay my debt to you. In fact, I don't feel that it's nearly enough. You didn't even ask for something for yourself."

Mina cast her eyes to the floor. She hadn't thought of anything for herself except for a way to lift the curse of the scale, but Klodian couldn't do that unless he killed the dragon responsible. And even that was only an assumption on her part.

"Is there nothing else that you desire?"

"I don't know," Mina replied. "Perhaps there is, but I don't think you can give it to me."

Klodian smiled knowingly. "If I could remove the scale from your leg, I don't know that I would do it. It has made me very wealthy."

Mina knew he hadn't meant what he'd said about giving her anything she desired. Aside from having the scale removed, the only other thing she wanted was freedom. And she knew with certainty that he wouldn't give her that.

"That is my desire, but I know you don't have the power to remove it," she said. "I don't think anyone does."

"There must be something else," Klodian pressed. "I do not want to be indebted to anyone."

Mina shook her head and opened her mouth to speak, but he silenced her with a stern look. She felt herself shrink before him. It was a habit, ingrained into her over the years.

"I had assumed you would ask for a few different things, and you surprised me by not asking for any of them. I've thought long and hard since we left the mesa, and I know what I will give you."

Klodian lifted his arm, his hand closed. It was obvious he was holding something, and Mina slowly moved her hand underneath his. Klodian drew his fingers back and dropped something cold and circular onto her palm. She pulled her hand back and saw it was a gold bracelet. Mina looked at Klodian quizzically.

"You are no longer a slave, Mina. This bracelet is a sign of your standing within my court. From this day forth, you are now an advisor to me."

"My Lord? I-I'm no advisor," she stammered. "I'm not wise in the ways of battles or politics. How can I be an advisor?"

"I will come up with a position for you, but until then, you are simply a member of my court now. You are free to come and go as you wish, but I ask only one thing."

"What?"

"That you continue to lead me to the dragons," Klodian said.

"And if I refuse to?"

Mina saw the slight clench in Klodian's jawline, but he surprised her with his answer.

"That is your decision. As I said, you are no longer a slave."

She was speechless. He had freed her. She searched his face, waiting for the reveal of a cruel joke. Klodian returned her stare, but there was no malice in his eyes.

"You are serious, my Lord?"

"I am."

"I don't know what to say. I ... thank you."

"You saved my life," he said. "There is no need to thank me. This is *me* thanking *you*."

Tears welled within Mina's eyes. She blinked several times, fighting to keep from full-on crying.

"There are some things I must see to, but if you need anything, ask the steward. I've already let him know of the changes, so you'll be well taken care of."

"Thank you again, my Lord," Mina said softly, still in disbelief.

She left the room in a daze and somehow managed to navigate the maze of halls to the servant's quarters. She walked to her bed, but something was different. A quick look around revealed that all of her belongings were missing. Panic washed over her and she looked under the bed. Her box of horns was gone.

"Your things have been moved to your new

room," Kera said from behind her.

Mina looked up at the girl from the floor. "My new room?"

"Yes. The steward had us carry it all. That little box with your horns has some weight to it."

"There are a lot of horns in it," Mina said. "Can you tell me where this room is?"

"Yes, but it's probably better if I show you. Come on."

Mina followed Kera into the hall and they turned left, leaving the servant's rooms behind. A few turns later and they entered the wing reserved for the nobles and other members of the court. Mina had only been to this part of the castle a handful of times, and she knew it was going to take some adjusting to the new surroundings.

Kera stopped at one of the doors and opened it, motioning for Mina to go inside. Mina did so, and she marveled at the expensive furniture and other trinkets that decorated the room. A sword hung on one of the walls, and Mina wondered what she was supposed to do with the weapon. Kera followed her gaze.

"This was Vhan's room," she said lowly. "The sword was his. The steward left it up, but if you want me to remove it—"

"It can stay," Mina replied, cutting her off. "I like it."

"Very well. Do you need anything before I go?"

Mina shook her head.

"If you do, ring the bell on the desk there, and one of the servants will answer your call. Sound travels oddly in these halls, so it may take them a moment to figure out which room it is." Kera paused. "Anyway, I'll see you around the castle, my Lady."

Mina squirmed at the last words, but Kera was walking out of the room and didn't see her reaction. Mina's entire way of life had changed so suddenly. It wasn't a bad change, but it would take her some time to get used to being referred to as "my Lady."

Windows lined the far wall, and Mina walked over to see what kind of view she had. The courtyard was visible, and she spotted a familiar figure. Caden. He was on a horse, riding toward the gate that led to his new life. Her heart broke at the sight of him leaving, but she knew that it was what he had wanted. She wished she could have said goodbye, but she supposed that would have been more painful than just watching him ride off.

She watched until she could no longer see him, then she glanced around her new room. She still couldn't believe that Klodian had freed her. He still wanted her help to hunt dragons, and she would gladly offer it. Until the curse was broken, she wouldn't stop tracking them for him.

The scene from the mesa flashed within her mind. The deep voices of the massive dragons echoed in her thoughts, and she knew it would be a long time before she forgot the sound of them. Mina rubbed the scale on her leg and looked back at the window. The dragons were nowhere near the castle, and yet she could still feel the powerful one. Why could she hear their thoughts? Why did she still feel the leader, even now? There were too many questions, too many things that she didn't know.

But she had an idea.

It was likely to get her killed, but if she succeeded, then perhaps she could finally be free. After night had fallen, she took Vhan's sword down from the wall and carried it with her as she quietly left the castle, heading for the mesa where she knew the dragon would be. She didn't know how to use a sword, nor was she strong enough to fight a dragon, but none of that mattered. She was going to get answers.

One way or another.

THE END OF BOOK ONE

ABOUT THE AUTHOR

Richard Fierce is a fantasy and space opera author. He's been writing since childhood, but began publishing in 2007. Since then, he's written multiple novels and short stories.

In 2000, Richard won Poet of the Year for his poem *The Darkness*. He's also one of the creative brains behind the Allatoona Book Festival, a literary event in Acworth, Georgia.

A recovering retail worker, he now works in the tech industry when he's not busy writing.

He's married and has three step-daughters (pray for him), a grandson, three dogs (huskies!), four cats, and two ferrets. He basically has a zoo.

His love affair with fantasy was born in high school when a friend's mother gave him a copy of *Dragons of Spring Dawning* by Margaret Weis and Tracy Hickman.